Grimaulkin Tempted

L. A. Jacob

Cover design copyright © 2017 by Niki Lenhart
nikilen-designs.com

Published by Paper Angel Press
paperangelpress.com

ISBN 978-1-944412-96-8 (Trade Paperback)

10 9 8 7 6 5 4 3 2 1

FIRST EDITION

Dedication

To Steven,
editor, writer, gamer, muse, friend.

ONE

THE WEDDING

I DON'T GET WHY PEOPLE CRY AT WEDDINGS.
My mother, I could understand. Probably tears of joy at seeing her only daughter in a dolled-up dress, with flowers in her hair. Possibly tears of sadness at seeing her only daughter get whisked away by a knight in a black tux, never to be seen again.

But that didn't explain the other people crying as my sister Evelyn walked out of the church, head held high, arm in arm with her long-time boyfriend Domenic Marcello.

I glanced at Scott, who unobtrusively wiped a tear from his eye.

"That was so beautiful," he said. He looked up at me, smiled and blushed. "Weddings are always beautiful."

"Maybe they'll let people like us marry someday."

He snorted. "Not in my lifetime."

I wondered, mostly if I could spend the rest of my life with Scott. We were still in the honeymoon phase; he still blushed whenever I touched or kissed him in public. He was more street-wise, more worldly than me; unlike me, who was stunted from prison.

We followed the people out of the church, and bottle-necked at the front while Evie was getting her picture taken with the wedding party in front of the church. I felt someone put a big hand on my shoulder.

"Hey, Mikey."

I turned around to see my cousin from my mother's side, Danny, He looked like a gorilla stuffed in a suit, with a thick beard and piggy-brown eyes. The suit jacket stretched to its limit across his chest, the shirt bulging beneath it. His tie was on tight, although I could tell that Danny probably was going to rip it off the first chance he got.

Next to him was a heavy-set woman who smiled at me. A pair of chubby children were at their legs, looking up at me.

"Hey, Danny," I said.

"How come you're not in the wedding party?" he asked me.

"I showed up too late to plan for me to be in the festivities."

"Where the hell you been? In the military?"

I thought that answered the question perfectly. "You could say that."

The bottleneck broke up, and Danny moved away. "See you at the reception!"

I turned to Scott, who smiled and nodded, and we walked through the open hole between people to Scott's truck. He'd gotten a new one after the other one got pelted with bullets. This truck was a Ford Ranger like the other had been, but black with red trim. I personally thought it had attitude.

"You know where this country club is?" I asked him.

"Not too far. I assume there will be a cocktail hour while the bride and groom get their pictures taken."

We got in the truck, and he reached down for the shifter that wasn't there anymore. I chuckled and Scott blushed. This truck was an automatic; its gears were on the steering wheel. He shifted it into Drive and pulled out of the church parking lot.

Evie and Dom had met Scott just two weeks before. I was afraid Dom wouldn't like him. It ended up that they were both Red Sox fans, so that was enough for Dom. Evie thought Scott was sweet. For some reason, that made me smile.

"You're still staying the night?" Scott asked.

"I hope so."

He smiled. "You're going to sleep on the couch?"

"That wasn't in my plans."

Scott said, "No hanky-panky."

"Scott, we've been going out for three months."

"And?"

He was more frustrating than a girl.

"I told you why."

He had been involved in an intense, loving, pure relationship about six months ago. The guy left for Toronto and never came back. Scott was still broken up, and didn't want to have that kind of relationship again any time soon. I thought he still carried the torch for the little shit. Of course, relationships in prison were a lot different than they were out here. Prison relationships were for convenience. At least Scott was being exclusive. That was a plus.

We got to the swanky country club. Now, although I was in a suit and tie, and was otherwise dressed up for the occasion, I didn't think that I belonged here. The whole setup made me uncomfortable. Scott was dressed up in a dark green suit, so dark it was almost black, even with a little light green satin kerchief in his pocket. He looked like he belonged here.

We followed a group of people into an area with tables, chairs, and a very crowded bar. Our table number was three; the one that held some of the bride's side of the family: my aunts and uncles on my mother's side.

I had always preferred my mother's side. They were Irish and Welsh, a strange mixture of booze-hounds and dry English wit. My father's side was all Norwegian and Dutch, not humorous at all. When you got my mother's side going, they were unstoppable in their drinking.

Dom's family was probably going to give them a run for their money. While my mother's side hit the hard stuff, Dom's family all had wine. Scott ordered a ginger ale, while I got a Diet Coke. We went over to our table.

Uncle Joey sat alone at the table, staring out into the room. I felt a pang of sorrow; he was Aunt Jane's common-law husband. Aunt Jane had "died suddenly", but I knew the truth: The Rosicrucians had killed her somehow. It was my fault. I tried not to let on.

"Hi, Uncle Joey."

He looked up at me, blinking. "Mikey?"

"Yeah," I said. I was going to get a lot of that over the course of the evening.

"How are you doing?"

He struggled to get up, but I ended up sitting down, Scott beside me. Uncle Joey dropped back into his chair. I suddenly realized that he had gotten old.

"Pretty good. This is my friend, Scott." I so badly wanted to say "date", but I didn't want to embarrass Scott or my uncle.

After nodding to Scott, he looked around the table. "I figured that Sue and Andy wouldn't be here."

Sue and Andy were his sister and brother-in-law; they belonged to some devout Christian church. At least, they did when I last saw them. Danny was their son, who left the church the second he turned 16. I remember vaguely the Christmas before I got sent away, that Danny wasn't allowed in the house. His sister Becky was still in the church, as I remembered. She was a thin, waif-like girl, not big like Danny, and she was very shy.

Speaking of which, Danny approached the table with his wife. The two kids had disappeared. "Mikey. Hey, Uncle Joey." He looked at Scott.

Scott rose, holding out his hand. "I'm Scott Angrier. I'm with Mike."

Danny hesitated for half a second. I knew what was going through his mind. He forced a smile and shook Scott's hand. "Nice to meetcha. This is Stephanie."

"Hi," she said, giving us a demure wave, before looking out at the dance floor. On the dance floor ran a gaggle of children playing tag or chasing each other on the wide wooden floor. That's obviously where their children had disappeared.

"What're you having?" Danny asked, looking at me and Scott.

"We're all set," I said as Scott raised his mostly-full soda.

"Uncle Joey?"

"Scotch and soda." He already had a full one in front of him.

"Hun?" asked Danny to Stephanie.

"White wine," she said. "And get ginger ale for the kids."

She gathered her dress under her and sat down. There was a seat between her and Scott, and two seats between Uncle Joey and Danny.

"It was a beautiful wedding," said Stephanie.

"Yes," Scott agreed.

The two of them fell into talking about the interior of the church, the beauty of the gown, and I was ignored. Stephanie warmed up to Scott by the time Danny returned with the drinks.

Then I saw a woman come up to our table. Her hair was pinned up in a tight bun, her make-up just so, not too heavy but enough to accent her features. She wore a slinky pink dress that flowed to the floor, but slit up the side about half up her thigh. She wore white high-heeled sandals beneath, and carried a white clutch with decorated sequins. She looked ready for a fashion walk down a runway, not a simple wedding. She was getting a lot of double-takes.

Danny walked up to her, giving her a kiss on the cheek. "Hey, Becky."

My eyes almost popped out of my head. "Becky?"

"Mikey?" she looked at me. She broke out into a grin and came over to me while I got up. She put her arms around my neck and gave me a kiss on the cheek. "I thought you ran away."

"I did, but I came back." I held her at arm's length and looked her up and down.

I must have looked too long, because Danny said, "Hey, they don't allow cousins to marry in this state."

I blushed; she blushed. With a grin, Scott handed up a handkerchief and wiped his own cheek with his other hand, meaning to me she must have gotten lipstick all over my cheek.

Becky said, "It's so nice to see you."

I wiped at my cheek, but she took the handkerchief and did it for me. She giggled when she did it. "Sorry I got you messy."

"That's all right," I said. I looked down to see Scott. "This is my friend, Scott."

"It's nice to meet you," she said, stepping back and holding out her hand.

Scott half rose. "Nice to meet you," he said with a smile. He shook her hand and we both sat down.

"How's your mother?" asked Uncle Joey, after Becky kissed him.

She shrugged. "Striving to make Dad be an elder. She's ambitious, but she says it's for the glory of God."

"Are you still talking to her?" Danny asked. "You're not an apostate?"

"Not yet," said Becky. "Though if she saw me like this …" She giggled and sat down next to Scott.

"What do you do for a living?" Scott asked Becky.

"I'm in training for medical billing."

"You should be a model," said Uncle Joey.

She giggled again.

Danny lifted his head. "Get Zach and Leslie," he said to Stephanie. "I see the bridal party out there." Stephanie got up and went out to the dance floor to gather her kids.

"What are you doing, Mikey?" asked Becky.

I shrugged. "I'm helping a private eye with some things."

"That must be exciting."

"It's been boring. Watching people." Nothing new had come up from Pawtucket PD, though I did get my money last week from the consultation I had done for them. I had gone on a few stakeouts for an insurance company, but nothing exciting.

Children started getting cleared out from the dance floor as I saw my father come into the room and go up to the DJ. My father and I had not spoken since that first day I saw him after I got out of prison. He always seemed to be busy, or watching baseball, or not even there. My mother would give me this sorrowful look, asking me to forgive him with just that look. I didn't. I felt I didn't need to forgive him. *He* needed to apologize for his behavior, not me.

The DJ began playing some slow music and started announcing the wedding party. They all entered and took places before the head table. Then we all rose when Evelyn and Domenic came in. They had their first dance, then the wedding party had their dance, and then they all settled in.

"Hm," said Scott. "They didn't greet the guests."

"Just as well," I said, glad I didn't have to shake my father's hand.

They immediately started serving lunch. The soup was salty, the salad bland and wilting, and the steak tarragon was nothing more than a chunk of meat with some salt and pepper. But the stuffed potatoes were to die for.

Danny said, "Evie's motioning for you, Mike."

I had my back to her, so I turned around. She was waving at me to come over. I got up and stood across from her, then squatted down so I was at her level.

"How's everything?" she asked.

"I hope you didn't pay an arm and a leg for the food."

"Too late now, right?" She laughed. "Listen, after the father-daughter and mother-son dance, will you mind if you danced with me?"

"I don't know how." My dancing consisted of boxing footwork.

"I'll lead," she said with a smile. "It's not complicated."

"All right."

After lunch came the required dances. Then the DJ announced, "Evelyn Marcello would like a dance with her brother, Michael LeBonte."

I got up. I expected the whole room to turn and stare at me. They didn't. Evelyn waited out in the middle of the dance floor as I crossed it. I had watched the other dancers intently, and saw that it was mostly standing around, shifting from foot to foot, without moving much. I stared at her awkwardly.

She smiled, and took my hands. Placing them on her waist, they started to play "Faithfully" by Journey.

"You know this song used to make me cry," I said.

"It made me cry after you left."

I looked down at the sequins on her dress. "You look beautiful."

"Thanks. I wish I could see you in a tux. You would have been more handsome than Dom."

I chuckled. "We can't get married. Isn't that still illegal?"

"It sure is."

"I see Becky filled out nicely."

I felt a tap on my shoulder. "Hey."

It was Dom. "Oh, you want to dance, too?" I put my hands on his waist, and guided him away from Evie.

"You're crazy, you know that?" he said, while I heard laughter.

"I've been wanting to do this since I saw you."

"Oh, really?"

I laughed to try and diffuse the situation. I let him go, brushed the front of his tux, and gave him a kiss on the cheek. "You take care of my sister."

"Or else?"

He knew the truth about me and hadn't mentioned it to Evie. His eyes were shining, from drink or from happiness, I couldn't tell.

"You know it," I said, guiding him back to my sister.

After the little dance with Dominic, I headed off toward the men's room. It went past a pretty big fountain in the middle of the lobby, behind which was another bar with men and some women lined up against it, talking and waving their drinks around. I saw Becky there, in the middle of a circle of men.

Becky had the helpless look of trying to be nice, but at the same time wanting to get out of a situation. One man had put his arm across from her, stopping her from leaving. It didn't take a mind-reader to see that she was caught.

Men's room forgotten, I walked over to the men. They were about my size, some of them a little broader than me, obviously men who worked out, too. The one who stuck his arm out had a paunch, but was broad in the shoulders and had a square Roman jaw — all the more easier to break if I had to.

"There you are," I said to Becky, and held my hand out for her. "I've been looking all over for you, honey."

She fell into the act as if it was second nature. She took my hand and the men surrounding her parted once they saw me take her in my arms and kiss her chastely on the cheek. I eyed the men carefully, daring them to try anything. So what if the suit Scott bought me would be ruined? It would be worth it.

"Don't forget your drink, babe," said the guy with the paunch, as he turned to the bar.

I raised an eyebrow. Before Becky could react, I took it from him.

"Thank you," I said, and with one hand at the small of Becky's back, I guided her away from the lions. I handed her the drink. "Are you all right?"

"Thanks for getting me out of there." She stopped, poured the drink into the fountain. I turned to make sure that the men were looking. They were. She left the empty glass at one of the pillars near the fountain.

"Who were they? Anyone you knew?"

"They kept calling him Mr. Carabesi, that one who gave you the cosmo." She shivered. "What a pig."

"Don't go around here alone, Becky. You're too beautiful for most of these Italian mobsters."

She laughed. "I can usually handle them, but he scared me, Mike. Especially with all his men around him."

"I'll protect you."

We went back into the main hall. "I can take it from here, Mike."

I smiled, and watched as she walked gracefully back to the table. Then I headed toward the men's bathroom. As I walked in, I was followed by two of the big Italians who had been with Carabesi. They watched me take a piss and, when I turned around, one of them pushed me up against the urinal.

We were alone in the bathroom, as far as I could tell.

Good, I thought, and looked at the man's hand on my shoulder, then at the man's face. "So what's this about?"

"You goin' out with that chick?"

"What's it to you?"

He shoved me again. I pushed against his hand, but he held me fast. Oh, well, I guess I was going to have to hurt him.

"You embarrassed Mr. Carabesi."

"I think he embarrassed himself, more likely."

I brought my hand up and grabbed the man's thumb, and yanked it back, hard — not hard enough to dislocate it, but enough to get him to let me go. The second guy moved, his hand cocked back to hit me. I ducked. I slammed my good left shoulder into the first guy, throwing him off-balance and into the wall across from me.

I could, if I wanted to, stand and fight, but that would embarrass my poor sister. Her own brother, caught in a fight in the bathroom with the in-laws would not bode well for the blending of a family. Instead, I dove out the door and slammed it shut, spelling it with a quick lock spell on the keyhole.

Whoever had the key would be able to open the door, but it was locked for now.

When I got to the table, Becky was packing up, taking her favors and getting ready to leave. "It's time I should go."

I looked at Scott. "Did you want to stay?"

Scott looked at Becky, then me. "No, I think I can go, too. It's getting dark and I have only one headlight on the truck."

We were in unfamiliar territory and, although I had put a spell on the truck to make the truck nearly invisible to police, Scott and I didn't want to tempt fate and get lost somewhere in the rougher sections of Providence with one headlight and no cops around.

Scott, Becky, and I found Evie and Dom standing with some people who were also saying goodbye. We waited and, when they left, Evie threw her arms around me and kissed me on the cheek."Did you have a good time?" She looked from me to Scott and back again.

"Yeah, we did." I patted her cheek. "Enjoy your first night together."

Dominic had that twinkle in his eye that meant they were going to practice making babies. "Oh, we will."

Becky gave her a kiss, said her goodbyes, and we waited for her.

I glanced at the men's room. A group of men had gathered at the door, trying to get it unlocked. "I'm going to walk her to her car," I said to Scott.

Scott nodded, walked a couple of rows away from us.

Becky threaded her way between Jaguars and Toyotas to her car, a Ford Taurus. "Thanks for everything," she said. "Can I call you?"

"Sure!" I rattled off my cellular phone number.

She took hers out and put my number in. She said, "Do you want mine?"

I nodded.

"Do you need to write it down?"

"I'll remember it."

She gave it to me, and I applied some mnemonics to remember the number, just like I applied them to remember spells and runes. I repeated it back to her, and she smiled.

"Wow, you must have a photographic memory."

"To a point," I said. I kissed her cheek. "Call me, we'll have lunch."

I returned to Scott as Becky beeped her horn driving by us.

"She's very nice," said Scott, getting into the truck.

"She's my favorite cousin. I didn't expect her to be so stunning over the past few years, though."

Scott chuckled. I got in and put on my seat belt. We rode home in general silence, listening to the radio, but not really hearing it. I was planning on how to get him into bed.

I visited his apartment once or twice, but never slept over. He lived on the east side of Providence, among grad students and other kids from Brown University. He rented the third-floor apartment, because he used the two extra bedrooms to store his inventory. This was different than most of the other apartments that were rented in this area. Sometimes they were three bedrooms but six kids to an apartment.

We parked on the street and walked a couple of blocks to his house. Even though most of the students were gone for the summer, grad students still lived in the area. During school days he had to park four or five blocks away and, if there was snow in the forecast, he had to park in a first-come, first-served parking lot a good half a mile away. But he loved his apartment and the old house it was in. He didn't mind the noisy neighbors, and it was within a short driving distance to his store.

I walked close to him, putting my arm around his shoulders. It was okay here, on the east side, since Brown University didn't mind openly gay professors and students. He leaned into me as we walked. I had everything planned. We'd start on the couch and work our way to the bed, stripping clothes off as we went …

"What're you grinning about?" he asked as he unlocked his door.

"Oh, nothing."

Honestly, we hadn't gotten that far, or even below the belt. He had seen me bare-chested that one time in his store, and I'd felt him up a couple of times.

There were five large rooms in his apartment. As soon as you entered, you were in his living room. There were two windows on either side of the room, one looking down at the driveway to the house next door, and the other looking into the third floor of the house on the other side. He had an air conditioner on the floor in front of that window, ready to be put in.

It was warm, but not stifling. Warm enough to be naked, I thought, and watched him go into the next room, the dining area. His bedroom was off that area, and there were two bedrooms parallel to a pantry. He went into his bedroom and kicked off his shoes.

My chance, I thought, and approached him from behind. I hugged him and he leaned back against me.

"Mike, I'm really tired."

"That's all right. We can just lay together until you fall asleep."

He shook his head, and pulled away from me. "I said you could stay over tonight. I didn't say you could sleep with me."

He pointed to the bed. "You can sleep in my bed. I'll sleep on the couch."

He'd said he wanted to take it slow. I wasn't used to this. I wanted to walk out on him, but I didn't want to lose him. He took a blanket and a pillow from the bed, and gave me a kiss on the cheek.

"Good night, Mike," he said, and closed the door behind him.

I fell face-first into the bed and inhaled his scent. That, unfortunately, would have to do.

I awoke to the smell of something burning.

Then the fire alarm went off.

"Shit!" I heard Scott yell, as I jumped out of bed.

I came out of his bedroom into the dining area to see a pall of very light gray smoke hugging the ceiling, and Scott waving his hand under the fire alarm in the kitchen to try and get smoke away from it.

I said a spell for a gust of wind and I blew out a breath. A breeze came from me through the apartment, dispersing most of the smoke and sending it to the windows. The fire alarm beeped a few times in resistance, then stopped.

Scott looked sheepish as he stood there in his bathrobe and a pair of shorts. "Sorry. I didn't mean to wake you up."

"Scott, I know you can't cook."

"I forgot about the toast," he said. "I think my toaster's broken." He went over to the toaster that he had unplugged and turned it over near the waste basket. Two charred black pieces of bread slid out of the toaster and into the basket. He wrinkled his nose.

"We can always go out," I said.

He nodded. "I think that's best."

He looked at me. I looked down. I was only in my boxers. I looked up and smiled at him. He was looking at what I had been looking at, and he swallowed.

"Um, let me get dressed," he said.

"Need any help with that?"

"I think I got it," he said.

"Uh huh," I said, still grinning.

He kept his head down and walked around me.

I had brought my backpack with a change of clothes, because I wasn't about to wear that suit again. While he went in his room, I went in the bathroom with my clothes and got dressed. We both met in the living area.

"Where do you want to go?" I asked.

"There's a few places around here. When are you going back to the apartment?"

"I told them I'd be back around noon."

"Gives them plenty of time to practice making babies."

I laughed as he got his keys and wallet from a bowl near the door.

I didn't know this about Scott, but on Sunday mornings, he preferred to skip breakfast and go right to Providence Flea Market. He suffered through a light breakfast with me, though, at Pat's Grill in East Providence, just across the George Washington Bridge. When that was over, and I could tell he seemed antsy, we went to the flea market.

Now, normally you think of a flea market as having a bunch of different people set up tables trying to sell old wares from their house. There were a few of those. There were also a few scavengers trying to sell things that they had found. There were also wholesalers, trying to dump new items at a cheap price.

Scott may not have been a scavenger, but I think I was a closet one. One guy had an old diving suit, complete with brass helmet. I doubt it really worked as a diving suit, but I was captivated by it. The guy knew I was interested, but Scott dragged me away.

"He's expensive," Scott said. "He'll bargain you out of an arm and a leg."

Some people even set up permanent booths. Most of them contained clothes and jewelry, but some sold produce and other non-perishable dented canned food. Scott walked past these with a determined air, and he stopped to talk to a couple of people in different booths and at some tables.

They seemed to know him, and shook his hand. One of the scavengers that he greeted looked me over and gave me a broad smile. He was from India, I think, with dark skin and small features. He had the lilting English accent, too.

"What are you looking for today, Mr. Scott?" he asked.

"Oh, nothing in particular."

"I have some of the pretty stones you like so much."

"Let me see."

The man looked around his wares, and then said, "Ah," and found a bag. Inside were raw stones, not even tumbled or polished.

"Two dollars," Scott said.

"There may be rubies in here," he said, shaking the bag. "I can't let it go for less than five dollars."

"I have to polish them all. Do you know how many are in here? Three dollars."

The Indian guy hemmed and hawed, but sold it to him for three dollars.

Scott peered into the bag when he got it. As he walked away, he said, "There's a lot of sea glass in here. I can use that."

We walked around some more. He stopped at a few other booths, while I looked over things like a tourist. I saw varmint traps (traps to catch rats, gophers, or other sort of pesky animals) next to new packages of women's underwear. Sponges and cleaning products near random household goods. I was glad when we left.

"That was worse than Wal-Mart," I said.

He laughed. "It's supposed to be."

We took a long, convoluted way back to Evie and Dom's apartment. We got there just after noon. Scott dropped me off, giving me a kiss, and I went up to their apartment and let myself in.

"I'm home! Get your clothes on!"

Evie said, "We're already dressed." They were sitting on the couch in front of the TV. "Our flight leaves in three hours."

"You all packed?" I asked, as I rubbed Rufus's head. He looked from me to the door. I was the one who took him out a lot, and I think he expected that since I was home, I was going to take him out.

Evie got up. Dom looked over the couch at me. Evie hugged me, saying, "I think I might have overpacked."

"How can you overpack for the Caribbean?"

"She thinks we're going to get malaria," said Dom. "Or seasick. Or both."

"I got the Dramamine," she said. "Just in case."

"Don't get off the boat, whatever you do," I said. "I read about how they treat tourists."

"We might not even get out of our cabin," said Dom with a leering grin.

Evie hit his arm playfully.

"I'm going to take out Rufus," I said.

I looked down at the dog and grinned at him. He knew what that meant, so he ran to his leash. It would also mean I got to spend quality time with Grimalkin.

I brought Rufus outside, across the street to the high school. Behind the high school was a line of trees that separated the high school parking lot from houses behind them. It was only about twenty feet wide or so.

As soon as I came within range of the parking lot, Grimalkin appeared beside me.

"Did you have fun?" he asked me.

"Fun yesterday? Yeah, until I got cock-blocked."

"You can force him."

I kicked a stone away while Rufus sniffed among the turf. "That's not what I want to do."

"You want him, you take him."

"You're not helping," I said, glaring at him. "The real world isn't like prison. There's more rules here." Unsaid rules. Culture rules. With liberty came rules.

Demons had rules too, and I knew them. They bound Grimalkin to me, after all.

Grimalkin suddenly looked out beyond me. I turned to see where he was looking, but there was nothing there.

"More come," he said, then disappeared.

I thought he meant more dog walkers, but that didn't happen in the time I was there. I brought Rufus back, and saw that Evie and Dom had brought out their luggage into the living room. They were going to take a cab to the airport so they wouldn't have to worry about parking.

Half an hour later, we waited outside for the cab. This was their first cruise: for two weeks, in a sunny, hot section of the earth, stopping in a few places on the way, but hopefully they would stay on the boat. I wouldn't know the first thing about saving them from Jamaica if the boat left without them.

"You have your bathing suits?" I asked.

"Of course," said Evie. "And the evening wear for the captain's dinner."

Dom rolled his eyes. "Another suit."

"I hope they have irons, or my dress will be all wrinkled."

"We'll just have to skip the captain's dinner, then."

"What? That's the highlight of the trip!"

"I thought being with me was the highlight of the trip."

"Of course, dear," she said, putting her arm around Dom's waist.

I said, "Evelyn Marcello. Are you ever going to get used to that?"

She grinned. "It does sound nice, doesn't it?"

The cab pulled up just then. She checked to make sure they had their passports, gave me a kiss on the cheek, and they climbed into the cab.

I waved goodbye, and off they went.

Two weeks.

I'd have to change the sheets before they got back.

TWO

MEETINGS

D OM HAD PAID THE RENT FOR THE TWO WEEKS, so I wouldn't
have to deal with the landlord unless something, God
forbid, happened in the apartment. Rufus looked up at me
when I came in.

"Well, buddy," I said. "It's you and me today."

I also had plenty of food — at least I figured I did. Scott
could always bring me to the store if I felt the need for it. I
made some lunch: pork chops with *au gratin* potatoes (I was
addicted to those, and boxed macaroni and cheese) and green
beans. Then I went on Dom's computer.

He showed me how to get online with AOL, America
Online. I had an email address. I called myself *Summoner88*. I
had no email except from AOL trying to sell me stuff. I went to

a couple of chat rooms, finding one on magic, but it was about rabbits-out-of-hats kind of magic, not my kind of magic.

I found out how much of a time sink the Internet was, because when I looked up at the clock again, three hours had passed. I sat back in the chair and looked at Rufus, who was lying at my feet, having little doggie dreams because I could hear him huffing. Or he snored.

I heard a chime, and someone sent me an instant message.

`hey`

Their handle was "*deomanking*".

I replied.

`Hey.`

`you play d&d`

`What's d&d?`

`lol dungeons & dragons`

I replied, after opening another window to check that out.

`No`

`ok bye.`

I frowned and looked it up. It was a role-playing game. I thought that was stupid. Why play with pretend magic when you can do the real stuff? I could create a "bag of holding" easily.

Another hour gone by.

There was no way I was going to spend two weeks on this computer, I thought, as I pressed the button to turn it off. However, it was either that or TV. Or call Scott every ten minutes. The library was closed, and I had read the books I borrowed for this week. They trusted me enough now to let me borrow five at a time. Even the ornery librarian didn't give me a dirty look when I said "Hi," to her.

Rufus got up when I did, looking at me expectantly. I pet him and said, "Dinner?"

He woofed.

So after dinner, it was TV time, and all I could think of was how bored I was going to be for the next two weeks.

⯌   ⯌   ⯌

Scott did not look his usual jovial self when I went into his store on Tuesday. In fact, he bit his lip, contemplating something, when I walked in.

I halted at the doorway.

"What?" I said, looking down. Was I unzipped or something?

He said, "I got a phone call."

"Okay." I closed the door and came into the store.

"From Tyler."

"Tyler …"

"My ex?'

"Oh," I said. I suddenly felt cold. "And?"

"He wants to see me."

"Does he?" I was pretty proud of myself. I didn't stop, I didn't pause, I kept walking up to him.

"I told him where the store is."

"Okay. When is he coming over?"

"I don't know."

I stopped in front of the glass counter. We had that between us. "So this means?"

He bit his lip again. "Is … are you okay with that?"

I wanted to say, *It's your damn ex, of course I'm not okay with that because I thought we were going out together.* "I'm okay with that."

He let out a breath. "Oh, good. I thought you would be mad."

"Why should I be mad?" I forced the smile. I was pissed. But I didn't want to lose him. I'd deal with the visiting ex — if and when it happened. I glanced at the clock on the wall. "I have to go back to the apartment and take out Rufus."

"Okay." He smiled at me. "Call me later?"

"Sure," I said. I hitched the backpack higher on my back. He looked up expectantly at me, but I turned around and left. It wasn't until I was down the street that I realized that I hadn't kissed him goodbye.

The phone rang at about 6:30. I was sitting right next to it and it made me jump. I picked it up on the second ring.

"Hello."

"Hi, um, is this Evie's husband?"

"No, her brother, Mike."

"Mike! It's Becky."

I turned the TV down. "Oh, hey, Becky. How are you?"

"Good, you're actually the person I wanted to talk to."

"Me?"

"Yeah. Are you busy? Can you talk?"

"No, not busy at all. What's up?"

I shut off the TV. Rufus, who lay on the couch with me, lifted his head, knowing that if the TV went off, someone was going to move from the couch. I just didn't want any distractions.

"Remember that creep from the wedding?"

"Yes."

"I think he's following me."

"Why do you think that?"

"There's this black car that keeps following me around. He's parked outside right now. I'm looking right at it."

"Becky, don't do that. Do you keep your curtains closed?"

"Yeah."

"Okay, do that. Stay away from the windows."

"Okay. I closed the curtains."

"Why do you need me?"

"You said you're a private eye."

"I work with one, I'm not really one."

"Oh." She sounded disappointed.

"Do you want me to see if you are being followed?"

"Can you do that?"

"Yes and no. I don't have a car or a license." The first was technically not true — I suppose I could have used Dom and Evie's car — but the second was definitely true. Nobody thought to teach me how to drive yet, and I had people to take me places right now, so it wasn't a priority. "I can talk to my PI friend."

"I don't know if I can afford a real PI."

"I'll get you a discount." I turned to the pen and paper that Evie kept by the phone. "What's your address?"

"1570 Main Street, Apartment 2C, Franklin."

"In Massachusetts?"

"Yeah." She chuckled. "Do you know of another Franklin?"

"No, no, I don't. I'll talk to Frank, see if he wants to drive out there. Tomorrow?"

"Sure."

"What time?"

"Uh … after ten. At night. I have to work."

"As a model?"

She laughed. "No, silly. At Stop & Shop."

"You need a real job," I said.

"As soon as I get my certificate."

"Okay. Talk to you later. Lock your doors and windows."

"I will. Good night."

I hung up and called Frank.

He answered, and I could hear a lot of electronic bells ringing in the background. "Yeah?"

"Frank, it's Mike."

"Hey, what's up?"

"I might have a job for you. Can you do a discount?"

"What kind of discount?"

"I won't take a cut."

"Keep talking."

"It's my cousin. She thinks she's being followed."

"How old's your cousin?"

"Twenties?"

"She live alone?"

"Yes. She's from one of those evangelist families."

"Jeez."

"And someone at the wedding came onto her. I had to save her."

"Could be either the evangelist group or a stalker. How are they following her?"

"She said it was a black car."

"That's no help. I'll meet with her. Can she come to the office?"

"She said she's working until ten tomorrow. She lives in Franklin."

"Franklin? Find out if she's available during the day. Bring her by."

"Okay." He hung up.

I debated for half a minute, then called her. She picked up after four rings, sounding breathless.

"Hey," I said. "It's Mike. Can you come here to Pawtucket tomorrow during the day?"

"I get out of class at two ... I have to be at the store for six ... yeah, I can do that. How about three?"

"Three it is."

I called Frank with the time, and smiled at Rufus. "We're back to work."

⛤   ⛤   ⛤

The next day I woke up and all I could think about was punching Scott's ex in the face. I didn't even know the guy. But he was already getting in the way of what I wanted.

I sighed. The outside world was so different.

Rufus slept with me and, as soon as I turned over, he huffed and jumped off the bed. After going to the bathroom, I got his leash and took him outside.

I got breakfast and settled down to read my newest book when my cellphone rang. It was Scott.

"Hello, beautiful," I said, answering it.

"Hi, Mike. Um … Tyler called. He's coming down today."

"I'll be in the neighborhood. I have a meeting with Bennett in the afternoon."

"I want you to meet him."

"Sure." I wondered if I could still punch him in the face.

"You sure?"

"Yeah. Sure, I'll meet him."

"Great! I'll see you later."

I hung up and looked at Rufus. "You know, I could probably beat the crap out of the guy."

Rufus looked up at me, giving me a doggie grin and wagging his tail. I laughed and scratched behind his ears. Dogs are wonderful.

I settled in again, and there was a knock on the door. Rufus barked, jumped off the couch and ran to the door. Confused, I went to the door. I put my body between the dog and the door and opened the door.

Standing there was a teenager, with auburn hair and dark blue eyes, a smooth round face, a little husky.

"Yes?" I asked.

He looked up at me. "Dom home?"

"No, he'll be back in a couple of weeks."

"My grandma needs help with something."

"Who's your grandma?"

He looked down and pointed. "Downstairs."

"Oh! Oh, sure." I pushed the dog back and stepped out of the apartment. "What's wrong?"

"Need to put in her air conditioner."

I raised an eyebrow. *Seriously?* I said, "Okay, lead on."

"Huh?" he said.

"Where is the air conditioner?"

"In the cellar."

Great, I thought.

I followed the kid downstairs to the cellar. There were three air conditioners down there. "All three of them?" I asked.

"I guess so?"

I went over to one of them. I blew the dust off of it and picked it up. I lifted weights, after all, so this would be nothing.

Okay, so it was a little heavier than I expected. The kid went up the stairs in front of me. I awkwardly had to feel for each step with my foot as I climbed the stairs. The kid opened the door into the apartment.

It was like walking into a museum of someone who lived in the 1950's. The curtains were lace and there were doilies on the kitchen chairs. I got to see the landlady up close and personal. She was shorter than the teenager. I had always seen her in the window. She had dark brown eyes and dark, Mediterranean skin, salt and pepper hair. She seemed surprised to see me.

"Where's it going?" I asked, trying not to pant.

"Come here," she said, with a Spanish accent. I followed her through the kitchen into the living room, where there were afghans and doilies of all sorts on the couch and chair. A thick recliner sat in a place of honor right in front of the TV.

She pointed to a window that was to the left of the recliner, and right in front of an old phonograph player, one of those huge ones that was the size of a cabinet. I put the air conditioner down on the hardwood floor and opened the window.

After manhandling the air conditioner into the window — it was pretty tight — she said, "Did you bring the sticks?"

"Sticks?"

"Jason, get the sticks."

The teenager didn't look happy as he left the apartment. I said, "Do you want me to bring the other ones up, too?"

"One. For the bedroom."

I went back downstairs to see Jason standing there with his hands in his pockets, looking at the remaining air conditioners. "What's wrong?" I said.

"I don't see any sticks."

I peered around the back of the pair of air conditioners and saw three foot-long sticks.

"This, maybe?" I handed them to him.

"Oh." He took them from me, and trudged up the stairs. I shook my head.

The bedroom was beautiful and smelled of roses. The light coverlet on the bed looked, again, like a museum piece, white with large pink roses. I put the air conditioner in, and she handed me a stick. I stared at it. "And I do what with this?"

She put it in between the top of the open window and the top of the window. She used the heel of her hand to bang it into place. She stood back, admired my handiwork.

"You're strong."

I smiled. "Yeah. I lift weights."

"Oh," she said. "Jason, you should lift weights."

Jason looked at the floor, flushed with embarrassment. I'm sure she wouldn't want to know why I started lifting or where.

"What's your name?" she asked.

"Mike."

"Thank you, Mike."

I took that as a dismissal, so I went back through the apartment and upstairs. Maybe she wouldn't look out of the window at me weird anymore when I went out for my morning jog.

I took Rufus out for one more walk, then headed to the gym. I worked out there and swam, killing time until after two, when I went to Bennett's office. I didn't stop at Scott's store as I usually did. I didn't want to get arrested for hitting someone before my cousin showed up.

Bennett was in his office, feet up on the desk, listening to talk radio. He had a frown.

"What's wrong?"

"This nutcase on the radio." He turned around and shut it off. "I should call in and give him a piece of my mind."

"That's what they want you to do."

He leaned back in his chair as I sat down across from him. "So tell me about this cousin of yours."

"I didn't see her much. Her father's some big shot in the church."

"What church?"

I shrugged. "One of those that don't celebrate holidays."

"Christian church?"

"Yeah, I guess so." They probably would have been impressed with me because I could quote the first chapter of

Genesis verbatim, but they probably wouldn't like to know why. "I get the idea that she left the church."

"And you had to save her from someone in the wedding?"

"Some creepy Italian guy."

"You better hope the Mafia isn't involved."

I gave him an incredulous look. "C'mon. Seriously?"

"Maybe I'm being stereotypical, but I'm sure not everyone in Dom's family is pure as the driven snow."

"Dom would know."

He only smiled. Someone knocked on his door and I got up.

I opened the door. Even in blue scrubs, Becky looked cute. "Hi, Mike," she said, and gave me a kiss on the cheek.

"Hey." I stepped aside to let her in. "Becky, this is Frank Bennett."

Frank stood up from behind his desk. He held out his hand. "Nice to meet you."

She shook his hand and I patted the chair across from him. "Sit down."

I walked over to the side of the desk so she could see both of us as she talked. She sat, holding her purse close to her.

Bennett asked, "Do you think you were followed?"

"I think so. But there's no parking outside. I saw the car pass by me when I came in."

"What kind of car?"

"Black. Four-door."

"Tinted windows?"

"No."

"Did you ever see who was inside?"

"A couple of times, there were two men inside. Today there was only one."

"Do you have a gun?"

She blinked. "No."

Bennett said, seriously, "I'm going to take you to a range and show you how to use one, and I think you should buy a Lady Remington."

"Frank, I could give her something not quite so lethal." I noticed the look of horror on her face.

"Magic?" he said.

"Yeah."

"Magic?" she said, looking at me.

"Something simple," I said. "A smoke bomb."

"Oh." She looked relieved. "I thought for a second you were talking Harry Potter magic."

"I am."

"Mike," said Bennett. "Let's get this straightened out, first." He got up. "Can you take us for a ride?"

"I'm sorry?" she said.

"Take us for a ride around the block. I'll tell you where to go."

She glanced at me to make sure it was okay.

I nodded and smiled. "It's okay, Becky. I'll be with you."

She looked at Bennett for a minute, then got up. She tucked her hand in her purse and pulled out her keys.

Bennett locked the door behind us and we went downstairs. I walked right past Scott's store, glancing inside as I did. A man stood inside there, but I couldn't see his face, as his back was to me.

Keep your mind on what you're doing, Mike.

Yeah, yeah, I thought, and followed Bennett and Becky to her car. I climbed in the back seat and Bennett got in the front, adjusting the side mirror so he could see behind us if he leaned forward.

Becky backed out of the parking spot and followed Bennett's directions.

"There he is," he said. "Black Lincoln Town Car, Rhode Island plates. Two men." He leaned back. "They're not even trying to hide, or they suck as tails." Bennett said to Becky, "Tell me about the church."

"Waters of Life?"

"Is that the name?"

"Yes. They're in Worcester. My parents joined it when I was really young. My mother's trying to make Dad into an elder."

"You left the church?"

"I'm leaving the church. Mom keeps trying to get me back whenever I see her. I try not to see her too often."

I said, "Frank, why don't we just see what they want?"

"What if they pull out guns?"

I rubbed my right shoulder unconsciously. It had healed, and I could lift with it, but it put in me a fear of guns. "I see that point."

"Guns?" asked Becky.

I couldn't see her face, but I could tell by the tone of her voice that she was worried.

"I don't think they're from the church. This has all the hallmarks of someone trying to scare you. Any ex-boyfriends?"

"Not recently. They're all in the church."

"What happened at the wedding?"

As Becky told him what happened, I started to weave a spell. I closed my eyes and visualized their car; something happening to their car to make them stop.

We turned a corner, and I heard a pop from behind us. All of us looked to see the car pull over.

"Go back to the office," said Bennett, as he glanced back at me.

I just smiled.

"Good," said Bennett. "We've got some time. Is there any way that you can stay with Mike?"

I blinked. "Frank, I don't know …"

"You'll have to put your love life on hold."

But Becky was shaking her head. "I have classes. And work. I don't want to put Mike out of the way."

Bless her heart, I thought.

"Thing is," Bennett said, "they'll fix whatever is broken and they'll be back at your house tonight. Stop right here." Becky pulled over, a block from the office. "I'll run the plates and see who might be following you."

"I … How much is this going to cost?"

"*Pro bono,*" he said. "You're Mike's cousin."

She smiled, and looked very happy — and cuter than usual. "Thank you so much."

"Don't worry about it. Mike'll call you tonight with what we find out."

We got out of the car, and she waved as she drove away.

Bennett hit my shoulder. "You didn't say she was cute."

"It slipped my mind."

I went up to Bennett's office and picked up my backpack.

"Going to see Scott?" he asked.

"Yeah."

He turned around. "Something wrong?"

"No, why?"

"You don't sound too enthusiastic. Don't tell me the glow's already worn off."

"I think his ex is there."

"I wouldn't worry. He's an ex for a reason."

"Yeah, I guess." He was right. I suppose I should be at least civil, then.

"I'll call you if I find out anything."

I nodded, and hitched my backpack on my shoulder.

I trudged downstairs and crossed the window of the store. There was a man sitting where I would normally sit, next to Scott at the side of the counter.

From what I could see in the window, he had dark hair and angular features. He was thin, a little taller than Scott, and was laughing when I saw him.

I could take him. No problem. I opened the door and turned on the "Don't mess with me" aura I had developed during my last two years in prison. This was after Grimalkin and I were training for a while, and I could feel comfortable about myself. And my place in the prison.

The two of them turned to me. Scott immediately blushed, as if looking guilty. The other guy's laughter died when he saw me. His eyes went a little wide. I could study his features now.

He had an oval face, a pointed chin with a very pronounced dimple. His eyes were dark brown in the florescent light. His hair was short, over his ears, which were close to his head. His skin was a little darker than my pale Nordic skin, and he reminded me of the Italians I saw at the wedding.

"You must be Tyler," I said, coming into the store.

Tyler got up from the chair. "And you must be Mike. Scotty was just talking about you." Tyler held his hand out. It was an artist's hand, no calluses that I could see. Long and thin like the rest of him. I could have probably fractured his fingers in my grip.

I took his hand and shook it firmly, squeezing just enough to show that I could beat the living snot out of him.

He took back his hand and I could see he was resisting the urge to shake it. He smiled at Scott. "He's pretty strong."

"I lift weights," I said. "I press 320." On a good day.

Tyler whistled in appreciation. Then there was an awkward silence.

Scott coughed and said, "Tyler told me where he's been."

"Ontario," he said. "Toronto. I'm a graphics designer."

"Are you going to stay in Canada?" I asked.

He shrugged. "I might. I'm there on a visa right now."

"You have someone there?"

"I did. He left about two weeks ago."

"Sorry to hear that," I said, not meaning a damn word.

"Thanks. I figured that was a sign to come back, to see how things are with Scotty."

"Things are fine."

"Don't think I'm trying to intrude on anything you two have," he said immediately.

"We parted as friends," said Scott. "He's still my friend."

If he's just your friend, then why won't you sleep with me? I wanted to say, but I kept quiet. I turned to Scott. "What're you doing tonight?"

"Tyler and I are going to the India," he said.

I hadn't been to the India restaurant with Scott. I tried to hide my disappointment.

I don't think I did a good job because Tyler said, "Maybe you'd like to come along?"

Scott whipped his head to Tyler. I noticed that.

"No, you two have a good time. Catching up." I started to the door. "I have to go home."

"Mike," said Scott, and I looked at him. What did he want? "I'll call you later?"

"Sure," I said, and left.

I no longer wanted to punch the guy in the face. I wanted him dead.

I walked into Bennett's office. "What's with the long face?" he asked me.

"Met the ex. They're going out tonight."

"Well, so are we."

"We are?"

"We're going to Franklin."

"What did you find out?"

"The car is part of a fleet for Herb Cadillac in North Providence."

"Who owns that?"

"We're going to find out." He got up. "First, to the library. Then to Franklin. We're going to tail the tails."

The library had access to the Internet. We walked up the hill to the library, and Bennett got in front of a computer. He started searching. "Herb Carabesi sound familiar?"

"Yeah. That's the name of the guy who creeped out Becky."

"Bingo," he said. "We should check and make sure it's the same guy." Bennett closed the window and signed out of the computer, but didn't shut it off. He sat back and grinned up at me.

"Let's go shopping for a Cadillac."

We walked into a pit of sharks.

That's what the salesmen reminded me of, as we parked outside and headed into the car dealership. There were four salesmen: two young and handsome, two older vets. They didn't seem to know what to make of us. We didn't look like father and son, and we didn't look like partners.

I didn't notice whether any of the men looked like anyone from the wedding, so I went to look at the nearest sports car. Frank split off from me, and the salesman followed him.

"Hi!" he said. He was older, about Frank's age maybe, distinguished white hair and compact body. "Can I help you?"

"I'm looking for the owner," he said. "Is he available?"

"May I ask who's looking for him?"

"He doesn't know me."

Meanwhile, someone decided to come up to me. "Want to sit in it?" he asked me. He was one of the younger salesmen, handsome and clean-shaven. His hair had a touch of gray in it. He had beautiful eyelashes with brown eyes, Italian olive skin. I'd do him.

"Nah," I said. "I'm just looking around."

"What are you interested in?"

I grinned at him. "Well, if I had to say so, I would like a Corvette."

Frank wasn't getting anywhere. The owner wasn't in the building. I walked around with the salesman. He asked me what color I liked.

"Red, I suppose."

"Red Corvette? We've got some of those."

Frank walked over to the service area and, while the salesman went to fetch a red Corvette for me, I went to Frank. On the wall in the service department were pictures. He was studying them, and I looked at a few.

"Here he is," I said, pointing to one picture. Carabesi, the one I had "insulted", was in a picture of a few people.

"He's not in any of the other pictures. I don't think it's the same guy. Ask your friend."

The salesman came into the service area and saw me. He smiled at us. "I've got a cute little number outside for you, sir."

"Could you tell me who this is?" I pointed to the picture with Carabesi.

He peered at the picture. "This is Herb."

I looked at the man next to Carabesi, and could see that they must be brothers. There was a distinct family resemblance with dark hair and eyes, even though my Carabesi was more tanned.

"I'll just need to see your license," said the salesman to me.

"I don't have one," I said.

His face fell.

I wanted to laugh. I patted his shoulder. "Thanks for getting the car for me, though."

"Mike," said Bennett as we climbed into his car. "You're evil."

THREE

BECKY

Bennett brought me to Evie and Dom's apartment and told me to bring Rufus with us. Rufus was notorious for getting sick in the car, so he stood with his hind legs on the floor, his front paws on my lap, and his head hanging out the front window. We drove to Franklin in the twilight.

I thought about what a great time Scott was going to be having with Tyler. And what would happen afterward. I didn't want to think about it, so I tried to pay attention to the talk radio bullshit that Frank had on.

"Why do you listen to this?" I asked him.

"Would you rather listen to National Public Radio?"

"What's that?"

"Classical music."

"No, thank you."

He chuckled.

We got caught in traffic around 495, and then it broke when we got past Foxboro.

In Franklin, we found one Stop & Shop. Frank was able to find Becky's car and parked a little bit away, among other cars. He handed me a five and said, "Go get a candy bar or something and go in her line. Tell her that we're here and we're going to follow her home."

I nodded, leaving a barking Rufus behind.

I went into the store, and scanned the cashiers. I saw her at number 12. I grabbed a Hershey's bar with almonds and got in her line.

She looked up at me, surprised. "What're you doing here?"

"On a job," I said with a smile. "We're following you."

She smiled back at me. "Okay." She handed me my change. "They're outside. I saw them when I came in."

"I know." Nobody was behind me, so we could talk a little. "Frank's on it."

"You're going to wait until ten?"

"Not any worse than some other stakeouts."

She turned and someone was putting stuff on the conveyor belt behind me. "I'll see you later. I really appreciate this."

"It's okay," I said, and left.

Rufus was in the back seat and jumped to the front when I came back. "No peanut M&M's?" he asked.

"You didn't say the candy was for you."

"Jerk."

I moved Rufus aside and got in. "She said she saw them when she came in."

"I've been watching the car. They went into Applebee's."

They came out of Applebee's around eight, and we watched them. Frank had to move the car because the parking lot thinned out and they were sticking out like a sore thumb, the black Town Car in the middle of the empty parking lot.

Just under two hours later, Becky came out. She came out with two people, talking with them. One was a man, who walked Becky to her car before continuing on to his own. Becky pulled out of the parking lot. Frank fell into place behind her, so he could see both her and the black car.

When she took a left, he went straight and took a left at the next street. The Town Car followed her. At the end of the street, he waited, but no Town Car came down the street. He parked the car at the end of the street.

"Take the dog for a walk around the block, see if the car's there."

I took Rufus out, and walked up the street that we had waited for the Town Car. I didn't see it, but remembered the name of the street Becky said she lived on. I saw it, a busy street with two sets of lights and parking on either side. I would look conspicuous with a dog on this street so I whispered the "don't see me" spell that encompassed both me and Rufus.

Becky's apartment was more of a duplex. Her car was parked on the street. Across from the duplex was the Town Car. Relying on my spell, I walked over to the car.

There were no lights over the car, but I could see two shadowy figures inside. Then the passenger looked right at me. It was one of the guys I had locked in the bathroom at the wedding. He had a look of surprise, and I realized that somehow he saw through my spell.

"Shit," I whispered, surprised as well.

The guy hit the driver's shoulder. The driver saw me, and he started the car. The next thing I knew, Rufus was tugging at me to go on a lawn while the car took off.

How did he see through my spell? I let Rufus take a quick piss on someone's fencepost. After Frank came around the corner, Rufus and I got back in the car.

Frank glared at me. "Nice job. You scared him away."

"Them. They're from the wedding."

Frank took off, heading to the highway. "That answers that, then. Dollars to donuts they're from the Mafia."

"Maybe I scared them away for good. They think I'm her boyfriend." I didn't want to tell him what was really on my mind.

They saw through my spell!

"I don't think so. You might have caused them to step it up. If these guys want something bad enough, Mike, they'll take it by hook or by crook."

I whirled to stare at Bennett. "How's that?"

"They'll try and contact her now. Tell her it's time to get the cops involved."

I turned to look out the window. Did I really just make things worse?

Frank got me back to the apartment around midnight. I collapsed on the bed, Rufus right next to me, licking my face.

"Yeah, yeah," I said, waving him off.

After a late-night snack for both of us, I turned on the fans and tried to settle into sleep.

How did he see through my spell? Was it the dog? I knew the spell worked when I held another object — there were plenty of times in prison when I needed to "hide" and I had books in my hand. Maybe it didn't work with a dog. Or a person.

"Grimalkin," I called, sitting up.

He appeared to the side of me, shimmering behind Rufus. Rufus, as usual, acted like he didn't see him.

"What happened?" I asked him.

He only shrugged.

"It worked in prison."

Again, another shrug.

He was playing hard to get. "Tell me, how could he have seen me?"

"He looked for you."

He was staking out Becky's house for *me?* "Why?"

He gave me an incredulous look. "Humans, like demons, carry grudges."

"Then why didn't he come after me right th—" I looked at Rufus.

Of course. Because of the dog. A big hundred-plus pound black lab with sharp, pointy teeth. Who was right now giving me a goofy grin.

I hugged him. "That's a good boy."

Grimalkin disappeared when I turned back to look at him, having answered my question. I sighed and got undressed, climbed into bed.

I dreamed of Scott. We were at a picnic in a park, one I'd never been to. It was by the ocean, because I could smell the sea. We sat together on a blanket, not touching, just looking out across a meadow and a clear blue sky.

Then he turned to me and held out a wooden chest, about the size of a box of cereal. He opened it saying, "This is for you."

Inside was old costume jewelry, gold chains, a wad of dollar bills held together with a money clip, and old yellowed envelopes tied with a ribbon. "What's this for?" I asked.

He just smiled — and something struck me on my side, pulling me out of the dream into a hazy half-sleep, when I realized that the dog kicked me. "Jerk," I whispered, hugged the corner of the bed, and fell back to sleep.

I checked for messages in the morning. Nothing. No Scott. It was Thursday, the day I usually went to the library to pick up my mail.

Jessica worked there on Thursdays, and she would secret my mail among the copies of the Congressional Record that the library got every Wednesday. If I had anything, which I hardly ever did, she would tuck it behind the stack of the Records and all I had to do was move them out of the way. Nobody — and I mean *nobody* — went to get the congressional records from Washington.

I arrived at the library with two iced coffees: one for her and one for Lillian. Jessica was at the desk and I handed one to her.

"Hello, honey," I said. She giggled and blushed. "Give this one to Lilly?" Lillian hated being called Lilly, so I did it behind her back.

"Sure."

I smiled and headed upstairs to the reference area where they kept the Congressional Records. I nodded to Jane, the reference librarian, who waved back at me. I went over to the stack of Records and took out the first few.

There was a manila envelope behind the stack. I took it out and turned it over. There was no address, but there was only one word:

Grimaulkin.

I felt a fire in my chest and I think my hands shook. I looked around, half expecting Ritter to be in the room. I checked to see if there was anything else. There wasn't, so I put the Records back and went over to a desk at the end of the room. It was in a patch of sunlight, so it was warmer than the rest of the room. I was nervous as hell when I opened the manila envelope.

I turned it over and shook out a bus ticket. I peered inside the envelope. A single 8"x10" piece of white paper was inside. I took it out carefully.

In the middle of the paper it said, "Bring me to The Arcade in Providence."

What arcade? I didn't know of any arcades in Providence.

Unfortunately, it wasn't handwritten, so I wouldn't be able to find out who sent it. I sniffed at the paper. It smelled like paper, nothing special. If I did a spell to find out if it was magic, it would destroy the paper, and it looked like I needed it.

I took the bus pass and put it in my pocket, then stuffed both the envelope and the paper into my backpack. I figured I'd ask someone who knew the area better than I did.

I walked up to the reference desk. "Hey, Jane?"

"Yeah?" she looked up from her computer.

"Do you know where there's an arcade in Providence?"

"*The* Arcade?"

The note did say that.

"Yes."

"It's the oldest indoor mall in the United States." She got up looked around for something, then grabbed a folded piece of paper. "Here's a map. I'll make a copy for you."

"Thanks," I said, and she turned around to the copy machine.

She made the map big enough for a legal sized piece of paper. "How are you going to get there?"

"Bus."

"Okay, take 99 all the way to Kennedy Plaza, then walk two blocks south. You can't miss it."

I used the bus pass and got on the 99 bus to downtown Providence. It was full, so I had to stand in the back. I glanced at the time on my phone. It was near lunch. I had a few bucks, so I could probably get something down in Providence.

I kept wondering who had left me this. Someone from prison, no doubt. It wasn't Ritter. Who?

Deposited at the bustling center of Kennedy Plaza, which was a hub of Rhode Island public transport, I pointed myself south and found myself facing a skyscraper. I looked at the map, and I saw I would have to walk around it.

It was the craziest set of streets I'd ever seen in my life. One building was a huge triangle shape, and behind that building, according to my map, was the Arcade. It was a three-story, wrought-iron building, with small, specialty shops on the bottom floor. The second floor had some stores, I guess, but most of them had curtains in the windows. The third floor was curtained off also.

If it was a mall, then it was going the way of the dinosaur. There were three cafes doing a brisk business, but the two clothing stores didn't look like they were doing anything much. There was a game store that looked interesting, but it was closed.

I wandered back and forth, not knowing what or who I was looking for. It started getting crowded around lunch, and I was heading out to the northern side, back to the bus area, when someone bumped into me. I felt someone place something in my hand.

I turned to look at him, but he kept on walking, getting lost in the crowd. I looked at what was in my hand: a plain white business card that said "Providence Atheneum" with an address. I fished out my map, and saw that the Atheneum was a building east of here. I had to go behind the courthouse.

I exited the Arcade and turned east, going past the triangular building, between two skyscrapers, and onto a busy street. I could see the courthouse from where I was standing. All I had to do was cross a busy street, a river, and walk up a steep hill.

Luckily, I was in shape, and there were crossing lights. I found my way to a stone building that was overgrown with trees and bushes, with a ten-foot tall dark green door. It looked like it belonged in a graveyard. There were no signs, nothing saying "Atheneum", but the map said this was the building.

I went up the granite steps and looked around the doorway. The hairs on my arm prickled when I put my hand on the door. There was magic here.

I pushed the latch and the door opened. It didn't creak, it didn't stick; it was a smooth, easy motion, well-maintained.

I stepped inside the cool, dark area, and could smell that distinct aroma of old books. As my eyes adjusted to the dim light, I could see the entire room was full of books. Floor to ceiling. With ladders. The bust of a man was at my right, and I turned to my left.

A policeman.

"Can I help you?" he said to me.

"I, uh —"

"He's with me, Sergeant," said a voice, and I saw an older, angular man with a cane walking slowly toward us. He had a wisp of white hair covering his otherwise bald head, and he stood straight up with the cane. He was taller than me, much thinner as well, and pale like a scholar.

The policeman nodded, and I turned to face the man. My heart started beating faster, more out of apprehension than fear. He had the pale gray eyes of a Rosicrucian knight, but he wasn't in the trademark black suit. He wore a tailored gray suit and tie, with a shirt that looked very light pink in this dim light.

"Please come with me, Grimaulkin," he said, and I could feel the tug of magic. *Trust me.*

I held my hand up in a protective gesture to ward off the magic.

He chuckled. "I do apologize. It's an old habit of mine. Please. Come this way." He started walking deeper into the library, not even looking back to see if I'd follow. I did.

Unlike the Pawtucket Library, this library was *old* — full of tomes with worn brown covers, smelling of musk and old leather. There were marble busts of different men every few yards. Above us a yellowed skylight reflected diffused gold light into the center of the building. The dim northern end showcased an unlit fireplace and six red velvet wing-backed chairs surrounding it, along with floor lamps illuminating the area in a sick yellow light.

He sat down with a sigh in a chair next to the fireplace. "Please take a seat."

I sat down across from him, placing my backpack at my feet. "What do you want?"

"Right to the point. I heard that you were quiet and observant."

"Life's different here."

"In the outside world, you mean."

I shrugged, looked around the room. I thought, concentrating, *What else do you know about me?*

He smiled. "I know many things about you, Grimaulkin. Such as your name. It's the name of a demon you believe you met while in prison."

"You're a Knight." Only Rosicrucian knights could sense uppermost thoughts.

"I *was* a Knight. I am now your parole officer."

"Parole officer? I thought that Ritter would have been that."

"Ritter is something else entirely. He was meant to put the fear of God into you."

"Yes," I said, thinking of Ritter. Funny, I hadn't seen him since … I had banished Belial.

"Did it work?"

I shrugged again.

"I didn't think so." He sat back in the chair. "I understand you assisted the local police."

"Yes," I said. "Ritter — the Knight who followed me — he knew."

"That is something normally taken over by the Rosicrucian Knights. He obviously thought you were capable and trustworthy."

Capable, maybe. Trustworthy? I doubted that. I had thought about it since that night. "I thought he wanted me to fail so that he wouldn't have to follow me around anymore."

He chuckled. "You seem to think that the Knights don't like doing their job."

"I can think of a few things better to do than follow me around."

"The Knights take an oath to protect the people from the unscrupulous magic users such as you had been. But you learned your lesson, didn't you?"

"Of course."

"Good. Because we can't let someone such as you go to waste."

"What do you mean?"

"What would you think about joining the Rosicrucians?"

Oh, no. Hell, no, I thought.

He raised a hand. "Hear me out."

I grabbed my backpack, but didn't leave.

"You would not have to take an oath, unless you chose to become a Knight. We have plenty of ways you could be useful, such as assisting the local police like you do now."

"What's the difference?"

"You would be working in an official capacity."

"In other words, I wouldn't get paid."

"You would be on retainer, of course. Your creature comforts would be taken care of."

"No," I said. "I don't think so."

He studied me, the way the guards studied me when Grimalkin stood in my cell, and they couldn't see him. The man tilted his head slightly, like a confused dog. "Are you certain?"

"Definitely certain."

He tucked a hand in his jacket, and pulled out a business card. "If you change your mind, please come back and bring this with you." On it was a sigil, one I didn't know. On the back was the name and address of the Atheneum. "Show it to the sergeant. He'll know what to do."

I put it in the pocket of my backpack. "Sure," I said and stood up. "Was that all you needed from me?"

He heaved himself out of the chair, obviously struggling to stand. "That is all."

I looked around the library. "Nice place here."

"You could use it at your leisure, if you joined us."

I laughed. "I knew you were going to say that."

The Hope Street bus dropped me off at home just after four in the afternoon. I took Rufus out and then called Becky, getting her answering machine.

"It's Mike. Call me."

I kept forgetting to use my mobile phone to call people. I considered it an emergency phone, something you used to call someone immediately. The phone at home was for everything else.

I made dinner, fed the dog, and then the phone rang.

"Hi, Mikey?" said the voice on the other end.

"Mom? Is everything okay?"

"Everything's fine." She laughed. "I'm used to a Wednesday night call from Evie."

"It's Thursday."

"I know. So … how are you? Did you like the wedding?"

I hated to have to get her off the phone. She sounded so lonely. We chatted about inane things: the food at the wedding, the weather, her car. Nothing about Dad. She knew better, I guess. She didn't ask much about me, and I didn't offer.

Half an hour later, I was off the phone. I sighed as Rufus lay his head on my lap and I scratched behind his ears, something I found out he loved.

The phone rang again a short time after I started getting into a book.

"Hi, Mike." It was Scott this time.

"Hey."

"I didn't see you at the store today."

"Something came up. How's it going?" *How's Tyler? Did you bed him yet?*

"It's okay. I was hoping you were going to show up today. Tyler wants to go to a club."

"A club? Really?" That was certainly not Scott's thing.

"I was hoping you'd want to go."

"Tonight?"

"Well, yes."

"You, me, and Tyler?" I didn't want to see Scott having a great time with my rival. "I'm sorry. I have plans."

"Oh." He sounded disappointed. "If you change your mind, we're leaving in an hour."

"I'll think about it," I said. I would think about it, but I doubted I'd change my mind.

"Okay, call me if you decide to go. I'll see you."

Going to a club? Not my thing. No sooner had I hung up the phone when it rang again. Finally, it was Becky.

"We know who's stalking you," I said.

"So do I."

"What?"

"They left roses at my door."

Bennett was right. They were taking things a step up.

"Are they still outside?"

"No. Mikey, I'm scared."

I sat up straighter. She was asking for help. What else could I do?

"What time is your class tomorrow?"

"I don't have class tomorrow."

"Can you come down here tonight? I don't have a way to get to you."

"Y — yes. Yes. What's your address? I'll get a map from the computer."

I told her my address. "Pack a bag for the weekend."

"Okay. Mikey. Thank you so much."

"Don't worry about it."

After she hung up, I looked around the apartment. I did hope to have someone over while Evie and Dom were on their honeymoon. I just didn't expect to be sleeping on the couch again.

Becky showed up around nine. She wore a tank top, shorts, and sandals, and looked adorably cute even to me. She carried a small suitcase.

I helped her with the suitcase and let her come inside. Rufus sniffed her and she smiled at him.

"Hello," she said to the dog, immediately scratching at his sweet spot.

"That's Rufus." I brought her suitcase into the bedroom.

"I'll sleep on the couch," she said, following me.

"Don't be silly."

"Don't you be silly. Dom and Evie are away on vacation, and you probably sleep on the couch all the time when they're home." She patted the couch that I had made up into a bed. "I'll sleep on the couch."

I was too tired to argue. "All right. Did you eat dinner?"

"I ate on the way. Do you have cable? HBO?"

"Uh … I don't know."

She found the remote on the coffee table. "I'll check, if that's okay? I really like *The Sopranos*." Then she bit her lip. "Maybe I'd better not watch it this week."

"Why would an opera be bad to watch?"

She stared at me for a second. Then she burst out laughing. I felt my face get hot. She finally calmed down enough and said, "It's a show about the mafia." She wiped her eyes, since she had laughed so hard she had tears in her eyes. "I don't need to see the stuff they do for fun."

"Oh, um, yeah. Okay. Right."

She hugged me. "I'm sorry. That was unexpected."

I put on the fans, and she stretched out on the couch. Any other guy, I thought, would immediately come onto her. I patted her leg and said, "I'm going to bed."

"Okay. I'll keep the TV down."

Rufus didn't follow me, staying with Becky for the night. Which was fine, because I got a good night's sleep without a dog kicking me in the middle of the night.

I awoke to my favorite smell, bacon. I smiled and turned over, getting up. Rufus came up to me, knowing that after I went to the bathroom, I would take him out.

Becky was still in her shorts and tank-top, cooking bacon in the microwave. "Good morning!"

"Morning to you, too. I need to take Rufus out, and I'll be right back."

So after our morning libations, during which I didn't get a visitation from Grimalkin, I came home to have a hearty breakfast of eggs, bacon and pancakes. "You don't have potatoes, so I can't make you home fries," she said, sitting down across from me with her own breakfast.

"What do you usually do on Fridays?" she asked me. "I don't want to get in the way."

"I go to the gym. I can skip it today."

"No, don't. Are there any stores near there? A mall or something?"

"There's a library."

"Okay, I can go hang out there until you're done." After cleaning up, we drove to downtown. She had to park in the public parking area and walk to the library, while I continued on to the YMCA. I decided to forgo the swimming for a shower instead.

When I left the Y, I went across the street to the library. I didn't have to go far to find her; she was in one of the wing-backed chairs among the newer magazines, looking through *Cosmo*. There was a pile of magazines beside her.

She smiled when she saw me. "Hey, let me just put these back."

I helped her put the magazines back and, when we finished, I stepped out into the main lobby.

To see Ritter standing at the desk.

"Shit," I said.

Becky stopped short. "What?"

Ritter was staring at me and Becky. Becky realized the man was looking at us. She looked at me, curious. Ritter came over to us. I started to try and walk past him.

"LeBonte," he said, calling me by my last name for the first time since I'd known him. I tried to walk past him, but Becky had stopped. I stepped back and took her hand.

"We're watching you," he said.

Becky was rooted in place. "What —"

"Come on," I said to her, tugging on her hand.

She finally started moving, and we walked through the doors to the outside.

"What's going on, Mikey?"

"Just come on."

I literally dragged her across the street, but she stopped when we got to the parking lot and yanked her hand out of mine.

"You look like you saw a ghost," she said. "What's going on? Who was that?"

I stopped walking, finally turning to her. "It's a long story."

She crossed her arms. "So start telling it."

What was I going to tell her? A lie? Or the truth? She stood there, waiting. I could lie. I could continue to lie to her, to my family. But I was trying to be good now-a-days. It was easier to tell her the truth.

I said, "Yes, I know him."

"From where?"

"Prison." I looked down.

"You were in prison?"

I nodded, still looking down.

"What for?"

"Magic."

She blinked, then forced out a chuckle. "You cut a lady in half or something?"

"No. Real magic. Like spells."

"There's real magic?"

I put my hands on my hips and finally looked up at her. "Yes."

"It's illegal?"

"Some of it is."

She came closer to me, put a hand on my arm. "Mikey, what did you do?"

I looked at her. "Summoned a demon."

Her eyes widened, but she frowned. "Oh, Mikey. Why?"

"To take care of things," I said. "I don't want to go into it." I pulled away from her and headed toward her car. It took her a minute to jump and follow me. I stood at the passenger side of her car and waited.

After a minute of studying me, she unlocked the door. "Will that man follow us?"

"He might turn up at inopportune moments." At least, he always had with me. "He's not after you."

"Great. I'm going to have a caravan of men following us."

I burst out laughing, then she started laughing.

"Oh, Mikey, things are too crazy."

"Welcome to the real world," I said.

FOUR

AWKWARD!

THERE WAS A MALL CALLED THE EMERALD SQUARE MALL about fifteen minutes away. It was built for the pedestrian in mind, with only one set of elevators at one end of the mall. The two main stores on either end had their own elevators and escalators.

We looked like a couple as we walked around. She dragged me into Victoria's Secret, jewelry stores, shoe stores, and clothing stores. I dragged her into the bookstore on the third floor, and found a curious novelty shop, Spencer's, that had some kind of inverted pentagram items for Goth posers. We ended up at the food court for lunch. I carried all her bags. This girl could shop.

I picked out some fake General Tso's chicken. Not as good as China Inn that Scott and I frequented, but it was at least edible. She sat down with a half-portion of *lo mien* from the same place I went to and a hamburger from Burger King.

We sat down with our food, and she asked me, "How does it feel?"

"How does what feel?"

"To do magic?"

"You really want to know?"

She nodded, took a sip of her orange soda.

I leaned forward. She did too.

"Like you're invincible."

She leaned back. "That's why it's illegal."

"Not all of it. Just the really powerful stuff that I did."

"If there's demons, there must be angels, right?"

"Yes, there are angels."

"Why didn't you summon them?"

"Because I'm not good enough."

"If you believe in Jesus, you're good enough."

I shook my head. "It doesn't quite work that way."

"Angels don't come in the name of Jesus?"

"No. Angels come if you ask them. Nicely. With pure intent in your heart."

She sipped again, thinking. I had dropped enough hints to tell her that what I did was not "pure intent". I wanted to kill people. Angels wouldn't do that unless they judged it to be righteous. Demons, once given the command, didn't judge. Angels had limited free will. Demons didn't. I learned that from an ex-Jesuit in prison.

"What was prison like?"

"Boring. Very boring."

"Didn't they have TV?"

"No. I had books."

"How long were you there?"

"Five years."

My sentence was probably for much longer than that, though they never told me. It didn't matter that people were dead. It mattered that souls the demon claimed — souls that could have gone to heaven — instead went into the demon's maw, and were destroyed forever.

"I would think you wouldn't want anything to do with books."

"I like them better than TV."

She looked up. "Oh, my God."

I turned to look in the direction she was looking. I didn't see any mobsters or anyone I knew. I saw a group of kids, a young man eating a pretzel, a girl talking on her phone …

"What's wrong?"

She was gathering her items. "We have to go."

I picked up her bags and she stood up, then she sat down quickly. "Too late. They saw me."

"They?"

She put her head down, her hand up trying to hide her face. "From the church."

I was standing and saw them, a pack of well-dressed young men and women making a beeline right toward us. The three men were in suits, no ties; the two women in demure soft-colored dresses. They looked like they were in their Sunday best. All of them carried booklets, and one of the young men stopped to hand out a booklet to a passing mother with a stroller. However, they were coming our way.

"Hello, Rebecca," said one of the women, about Becky's age, a little more stocky, smiling sweetly. In fact, they all were smiling sweetly at me. It was creepy.

"Hi, Estelle."

"Who's your friend?"

"Mike," I said, holding out my hand. She put her hand in mine, like a limp fish.

"Would you like to hear the Good News of the Lord?"

"I already have, thank you." I bent and picked up the bags. Yes, they were from Victoria's Secret and The Gap, so they certainly weren't for me. And Becky was in her tank and shorts, definitely not like the church-going young people standing before me. Becky was red-faced as she stood up.

The other girl said, "We've missed you at church."

"I've been busy. School. Work."

"Working on the Sabbath is not what the Lord wants," said one of the men.

"Working on the Sabbath in the service of the Lord is what He wants," continued another.

"However," I said, "God gave you free will before He gave you the Commandments."

The sweet smiles disappeared. Becky put her hand on my arm. "We have to go," she said.

"Don't stray too far from the Lord," said Estelle. "Or you'll never find your way back."

I followed Becky's lead and went to the escalators.

We walked to her car in silence. It wasn't until she got into the car that she started to cry quietly, tears rolling down her cheeks.

"Hey, now," I said, putting my arm around her shoulders and pulling her to me.

"They're going to tell my mother," she sobbed. "They're going to say I looked like a slut and I was with a boy. My mother won't talk to me anymore and they'll kick me out like they did with Danny."

"Danny seemed to do all right for himself."

She shook her head, pulled back. "All the horrible things they said about him. And then it was like he never existed. We never spoke about him in the house again." She sniffled. I opened the glove box and found a napkin, giving it to her. "I'm an apostate," she said, after blowing her nose. "Mom might try to call me, to get me back. She'll say it's the school's fault and won't pay for it anymore."

"You're starting to panic," I said. "Take a deep breath with me. In."

I breathed deep. She copied me.

"Out."

We exhaled together.

"Good. Better?"

She nodded, wiped her eyes. "I'm sorry."

"What for? You can't help that you know people who are jerks." I patted her leg. "Let's go back to the apartment. Or we can rent a movie."

"Yeah, the apartment."

I didn't even get two steps up when the door downstairs opened.

"Mike?" called the landlady.

Becky stopped at the top of the stairs. I waved my hand to her, then came downstairs to see the landlady. "Yes?"

"Can you help with the other air conditioner?"

"Sure," I said. I tossed the apartment key to Becky, saying, "I'll be right up."

I went downstairs in the cellar to the other air conditioner. It was a little bigger and more awkward than the other two A/C's I brought up. I had to turn it sideways to get it through the door.

She stood at the window I was going to put the air conditioner in. It was a large window, facing out onto the porch. I put the air conditioner in, and turned to see the landlord sitting in his chair in the living room. She put the stick in the window and plugged it in.

"Thank you," she said.

"No problem," I said, wiping my face. It was warm in here. I could imagine what it would be like upstairs.

Rufus greeted me at the door when I got there, doing his pee-pee dance, going around and around at the door. It was hot in the upstairs apartment.

"Becky, I'm taking Rufus out."

"Okay!" I heard her call from the bathroom.

"Put the fans on, okay?"

"Okay!"

I grabbed the leash and brought Rufus out. We walked around the block. It wasn't hot, but it was uncomfortably warm by the time we got back. Rufus drank water while I went to the bathroom.

When I came out, Becky stood in the living room in a pink lace bra and black panties.

"What do you think?" she asked me. She turned her torso to the right, so I could see the lace on her bra.

"It's nice," I said. Any other man, I knew, would tackle her and get underneath the underwear.

She turned to face me. The bra brought together and pushed up her breasts so there was deep cleavage. I walked by her to the windows, and put on the fans, but closed the shades half way down out of modesty.

She stared at me while I did that and, when I finished, she said, "Do you think I'm pretty?"

I was sweating from the heat, not from attraction. "I think you're beautiful, Becky."

"Then …"

"Then, what?"

Then, the phone rang. I walked across the room and picked it up. "Hello?"

"Hey," said Scott.

"Hey, Scott."

He was silent for a minute. "Want to go out tonight?"

"I have a guest. Where do you want to go?"

"Tyler wants to —"

I didn't hear the rest. That little jerk was still around. When was he going to leave?

"I'm sorry," I said, when there was a pause in the conversation. I honestly hadn't heard a bit of it. "Like I said, I have a guest."

Meanwhile, Becky had gone into the bedroom and came out in her tank and a pair of shorts. She heard me and said, "Don't not go anywhere on my account."

I waved a hand at her, dismissing the idea. Then Scott said, "Please, Mike?"

Please? How could I say no? Becky went into the kitchen and was making something, Rufus following her to pick up scraps.

"Okay," I said. "I'll go."

"Great, I'll pick you up in half an hour."

After I hung up, Becky came out of the kitchen. She smiled at me, saying, "It didn't hit me until I heard you on the phone."

"What didn't?"

"You're gay, aren't you?"

"Yes. Is that a problem?"

"No! You were being honest. About me being beautiful."

"Of course I was being honest."

I walked up to her and gave her a hug. She hugged me back, fiercely. "I love you so much, Mikey."

I chuckled, gave her a kiss on the cheek. "I love you, too."

She patted my arm. "Now go get ready for your date."

I wore a black t-shirt, jeans and sneakers. Becky settled in with pizza, TV, and Rufus. I gave her a quick kiss on the cheek and went downstairs to wait for Scott.

Scott pulled into the driveway. Tyler didn't get out of the truck, instead moving closer to Scott.

"Hey," Tyler said, giving me what he probably thought was a winning smile.

"Yeah," I said, getting into the truck. Tyler sat really close to Scott, almost on his lap.

"I didn't realize it was going to be this tight," said Scott, pulling away. "Maybe we should go back to the house and get your car, Tyler."

"But I don't know where I'm going," he said, putting an arm around Scott's shoulders.

"I'll drive it," said Scott, glancing at me. He looked away quickly. I suppose I didn't have the most pleasant of looks on my face.

I asked, "How far is this place?"

"It's Tortilla Flats."

"We can walk to it from your house, Scott."

Tyler frowned. "Isn't it on the way home?"

Scott sighed. "All right, all right. It's only down the street."

Tyler stretched his leg out, placing it on top of mine. He didn't move when we touched. He just grinned.

Among the things going through my mind were, *Are you kidding me? You're flirting with me, with Scott right there?*

I didn't move.

Tyler said to me, "I was hoping I'd get some time to talk to you before I left." He put his arm up on the seat, his hand close to my shoulder.

"When are you leaving?"

He looked at Scott. "Oh, I don't know, maybe next week?"

I looked at Scott, too. He had on his poker face. That meant he wasn't happy about the idea.

Tyler smiled at me. "I've heard a lot about you."

"Have you."

Scott waited at the light near the restaurant. It didn't look like there was any parking nearby.

"I heard you do magic."

"Yes, I do." Scott turned the corner, and found a parking space a block away from the restaurant. I hoped Scott didn't go into detail.

"Real magic? Like what Scott's into?"

"Sort of."

"What do you do?"

I climbed out of the truck as soon as Scott finished parking. Tyler pulled his arms down and scooted out of the truck on my side. I shut the door, while Scott locked it remotely.

"Do they have watermelon margaritas?" asked Tyler as we crossed the street.

The sidewalk was wide enough for us to walk three abreast, so I didn't have to jockey for position next to Scott. We congregated at the door, and Tyler held it open for Scott and me.

The place was crowded. It was after six, when the dinner crowd was probably coming in. I made a point to sit next to Scott, and Tyler climbed into the booth across from us. After settling in, Tyler picked up the liquor card and perused the cocktails.

"Hello, boys," said our waitress, putting down cocktail napkins. "We have a special on mango-ritas."

"Got any watermelon ones?" asked Tyler. I looked at the menu over Scott's shoulder.

"Sure, hon," she said. "I'll have to see some ID's, first."

Tyler tucked into his back pocket and pulled out his wallet. He showed her his driver's license. I noticed it said Massachusetts.

The waitress nodded and asked, "Want sugar or salt?"

"Sugar."

"You got it." She turned to us.

I said, "Diet Coke."

Scott said, "The same."

She nodded and threaded her way between booths and tables to the bar.

I wasn't well-versed in Mexican cuisine, but I did know what tacos were. They had those at the prison. I learned not to question what the ground meat was.

I decided on a loaded chicken burrito. Better to be safe. Scott got something else, while Tyler got a combo platter.

After our drinks arrived and the waitress took our orders, Tyler said to me, "You didn't answer my question from earlier."

"What's that?" I said.

"What kind of magic do you do?"

Either Scott didn't tell him, or Tyler wanted to hear it from the horse's mouth. So I decided to give him something to chew on.

"Tantric magic."

Scott choked on his soda.

Tyler looked at him sharply, and then looked at me. "What's that?"

I raised an eyebrow. "You mean Scott hasn't told you what Tantric magic is? I practice it all the time. Scott, why don't you tell him?"

Scott was blushing bright red. He said, without looking at either one of us, "Um, it's sex magic."

"Well," I said, getting all pedantic on them, "It's more than just 'sex magic'. It's the raising of power through sex or masturbation in order to cast spells."

Tyler said, "Wait, wait … you have to masturbate to cast a spell?"

"That's right."

"Any spell?"

"Any spell."

"Like, if you wanted to cast a spell right here, you'd just whip it out and —"

"I can prove it." I put both hands under the table.

The look on Tyler's face was priceless.

Scott put a hand on my arm, "Maybe not right now," he said. I shrugged and brought both hands back up on the table.

Was Scott trying to defuse the situation, participate in my role-play, or what?

I sipped my soda, then asked, "So what brings you from Toronto?"

"Oh, I …" Tyler pulled himself together. "I wanted to see how Scott was doing."

"You could have just called."

"It's not the same." He smiled at me. "And to see who he hooked up with."

"So you see me."

The silence fell on the table with a thud. We all drank.

Scott said, "Tyler's a graphic artist."

"What exactly is that?" I asked.

"I make logos for people. Scott and I are trying to develop one for his store."

Scott said, "I was thinking oceans or water and maybe a Chinese character for Reiki or something."

"You're not anywhere near the ocean."

"This is the Ocean State."

"If you were near the ocean, I could see that. But you're in the middle of a city. I think a symbol of the triple goddess with a wave splitting it in half, and have the top of the symbol reversed from the bottom."

"Why not a white raven?" I said. That was the name of his store, after all.

They stared at me like I didn't know what I was talking about. "Crows and ravens are a dime a dozen for pagan stores," said Scott.

Tyler shook his head. "Besides, you want a symbol, something unique."

So I shut up and let them discuss it. The discussion continued over dinner, with Tyler drawing things on napkins. Scott didn't seem happy about anything Tyler was coming up with. I didn't like anything either, but I was biased.

Finally, Tyler sat back from the table, his margarita finished a long time ago. Nothing remained on his plate, not even a speck of lettuce. I had gotten a refill on my soda while eating. Scott was done with his dinner and soda, and now we had to split the bill.

"My treat," said Tyler.

"Okay," I said, putting my wallet back in my pants pocket. Scott gave token resistance but he, too, put his wallet back.

Outside, Tyler said something to Scott, who then looked behind him at me.

"Ask him," Scott said, and walked on ahead.

Tyler put a hand on my shoulder. "Hey, we can walk back to Scott's place and meet him there. I want to talk to you, privately."

Scott was already halfway to the truck. He turned around for a moment to see the two of us walking together. Tyler made a motion, as if to shoo him away. Scott shrugged and continued to the truck.

I didn't want him to go. But if Tyler wanted to talk, he must have something important to say.

"Okay," I said and started walking down the street, away from the truck. Tyler jumped to catch up.

"Slow down, Mike," he said.

So I did, and waited for him to walk side by side with me. Scott and his truck went past us as we walked the four or five blocks to his house.

"What is it that you want?"

"I get the feeling that you don't want me around."

"Gee, whatever gave you that idea?"

"You've been avoiding us."

"Something came up."

"Scott said you were going to sleep over."

"That was before I had my cousin over."

"I was hoping you would sleep over."

I stopped short. "What?"

He stopped with me. "Sure. The three of us. You know."

Let me tell you a little thing about prison relationships. Gang rapes are not that uncommon. Having been the victim of a couple before I got the power and respect enough to fight them off, I didn't like any more than two people having any kind of sex. I didn't like kinks, I didn't like receiving, and I certainly didn't like more than one person's hands on me.

"No," I said, in what I hoped was my most firm voice. "Absolutely not."

"C'mon, man."

That made me even more angry. I could barely restrain myself from throwing him into the nearest car. "I have more respect for Scott than that."

"Scott would love it."

"He's not a toy to be used like that."

"It'll be fun —"

That's when I grabbed him by the front of his shirt and yanked him toward me. "Listen here, Tyler. He's *my* boyfriend. If you've been having sex with him then I swear to the gods I will kill you."

Tyler's wide-eyed look of fear was almost enough for me. I wanted him to wet his pants, that's how angry I was.

"Are you having sex with him?"

"No, man. No."

I released him.

"I thought … I thought that he would, if it was okay with you, and the three of us —"

"It's not okay with me. To tell you the truth, I really don't like you, Tyler."

He brushed at his chest. He wouldn't look at me, which was just as well.

"I'll walk you back to Scott's house and then I'm going home." I leaned in close. "And shut up."

He started walking. I walked beside him, in my own thoughts. I would kill him, no doubt about that. I assumed they were having sex, and that would have been my excuse to kill him. He was a shadow, in the way. I had the power to do it. I could do it. I *would* do it.

And if I did it, I would be back in jail so fast that nobody would know what happened.

We were in front of Scott's house when I said, "Go."

Tyler, his weasel head hung down, trudged up the walkway to the door. I turned around and started home, which was at least a two or three miles away. Not really that far. The night was warm but not hot, and I'd walked longer distances. It's just this way had hills and valleys.

I had gotten past Tortilla Flats and was approaching the businesses near Rochambeau when I heard a beep. I turned to the street and Scott was in his truck, alone.

"Get in," he said.

I did. He didn't look happy.

"You could have at least come upstairs. I would have given you a ride home."

"Let me guess," I said, "Tyler told you I threatened him."

At the stoplight he turned to me. "That explains his expression when he walked in the door."

"Did he tell you why?"

"I didn't get a chance. You're going to tell me why, right?"

"He wanted a threesome."

Scott turned away from me when the light turned green. He looked confused. "The three of us?"

"And he said you weren't having sex. I thought you were."

He sighed. "Mike. I've been trying to get rid of him this whole week and was hoping you'd come with us to get him to stop coming onto me."

"I — I thought you two were …"

He shook his head. "I'm over him. I've been over him. This is the last straw."

"You don't want a threesome?"

"No!" he said. "Not with him, anyway."

I looked out the window. "He made assumptions."

"They're wrong. I'm not the same person. Mike. If I'm going to have sex with anyone, it would be with you."

I whipped my head to face him, but he was concentrating on driving. I wanted to ask, *Then why won't you?*, but I didn't want to ruin the moment. I was at least smart enough to do that.

We were silent for the rest of the ride to my house.

He dropped me off and said, "Will you help me get rid of him?"

I nodded.

"I'll call you tomorrow. Bring your cousin. Is it a guy?"

"No."

"Good. It might put him on his best behavior."

I got out of the truck, and he pulled away.

I went upstairs, and Becky was still awake.

"You're home early," she said, as Rufus jumped off the couch and came running up to me.

"It didn't quite work out," I said. "I'm going to take Rufus out."

"Okay," she said from the couch.

I brought Rufus to the small woods behind Hope High School and called for Grimalkin. I heard the sound of horns in my mind, loud and obnoxious and not playing music that humans would enjoy.

They were the harbingers of Belial.

FIVE

SPELLWORK

I DIDN'T HAVE TIME TO PUT UP A PROTECTIVE CIRCLE. Rufus tugged at the leash, having caught the scent of something interesting. I yanked Rufus to me and started praying "Our Father".

Belial appeared before me, not unlike how Grimalkin does, a couple of yards away from me. He laughed at my paltry attempt to protect myself. But he wasn't solid like he had been the last time I saw him. He seemed to be half-in, half-out of a nearby tree and his feet didn't touch the ground. He wore full black armor, including a helmet that emphasized his fiery yellow eyes.

I made a protective motion with my hand, the most powerful one I could think of, and I could see the shield come up between us, encompassing Rufus and I. Rufus didn't see

Belial, but he sat down obediently when I tugged his leash downward.

"So you want to kill someone again."

"No," I said to Belial. "I want to be rid of him. I didn't summon you."

"You summoned what is most powerful within you."

Within me? Oh, no.

"Oh, yes. I live within you, wizard. I know your thoughts, your desires." He floated on the air toward me. "I can help you attain those desires."

"In exchange for what?"

"My only satisfaction is to see you become powerful. You have the right — and the ability — to become the most powerful wizard in the world."

"With your help, of course."

"Of course."

"The Knights will see right through it."

"You are beyond even the ability of the Knights to see."

"If I use your magic, they'll know and they'll arrest me. I'm surprised they're not here now."

"You are not using *my* magic. You are using your own."

I didn't like this arrangement. Something felt wrong. The Rosicrucians would find out and I would be screwed. But if he was just going to give me the spell, I would use my own will to make it work.

"Then tell me."

He did. It was so simple, an apprentice could do it. As soon as he told me, he disappeared, so I couldn't ask questions. I was thinking, *What a jerk,* but the spell was simple to remember.

When I got home, I went right to the kitchen and gathered the items for the spell. Becky was in the bathroom, and I finished just as she came out.

"I have to go to work tomorrow," she said. "From three to nine."

"Okay. The guys wanted you to come along tomorrow. I don't know what their plans are." If I had my way, Tyler wouldn't be coming. "I'm going to bed," I said, taking implements with me.

I went in the bedroom and did something unusual. I kicked out Rufus.

I took the fan out of the window. It was stifling hot. I didn't know where the air conditioners were so I couldn't put them in. Poor Becky was going to need a shower in the morning because of the heat tonight, if she could sleep.

I had two white candlesticks in my hand. I lit a match and set one candle alight. I let some wax drip onto the window ledge, and then placed one candle in the puddle. It stood up. I did the same thing for the other candle, and set it down to the first candle's left. I put them both close together, but not touching.

"By my will," I said, pinching the second candle at its base. "By my will within seven days, you shall leave this place, never to return."

I dragged it away from the first candle, just an inch away. I concentrated on it, envisioning Tyler in the flame, as the flame fluttered and spat. There was resistance.

I poured my will into the spell. "Seven days. You will leave within seven days."

The flame continued to burn, faster than the first candle. I was sweating, from the heat or the force of my will, I don't know which. Regardless, I watched as the second candle burned half-way down, while the first candle was still and serene, its flame burning merrily.

I pinched both candles out, and turned to the second candle. Belial said to break it. I knew what would happen if I did.

Tyler would probably die.

Instead, I took down both candles. Keeping them separate, I lay one candle on the nightstand, and I threw the half-burned candle in the trash.

Becky, if left to her own devices, admitted to being a couch potato. I had to almost drag her out of the apartment to the gym.

I was able to get her into the aerobics class (it helps when Dom works there and doesn't utilize most of the services) while I did my workout. She hadn't brought a suit, so came into the pool area after a shower and sat in the bleachers.

She called to me at one point, "Mike, you have a call."

I hauled myself out of the pool and, dripping wet, walked up to her. She handed me a towel, then the phone.

"Hello."

"Hey," said Scott. "We're thinking of going clubbing tonight."

"Scott, I don't have an ID."

"That's okay. They don't card you at this place we went to."

Becky said, "You want to go out, go ahead. I'll go home tonight."

"Are you sure?" I said to Becky.

She smiled. "I'm sure it's okay now."

"All right," I said into the phone. It was Friday. It would be busy. But I knew I could get in, no problem.

"Great! I'll see you around nine. We'll be taking Tyler's car."

"Okay," I said, and hung up. I handed the phone back to Becky. "You sure you're going to be all right?"

She nodded. "It's been two days."

I gave her a quick peck on the cheek. "Let me go get dressed."

It was about one when she dropped me off at the house. I noticed a silver car parked behind Dom and Evie's car. A huge car, its trunk hung out onto the sidewalk and its front bumper touched Dom and Evie's car.

"Call me when you get to work," I said. "And call me when you get home tonight."

"You'll be in a bar. You won't hear the phone."

"It'll be in my pocket. It shakes."

"Vibrates," she said with a giggle. "It's called 'vibrate'."

"Okay, okay. Call me!"

She drove away and I waved. I looked at the silver car. I hoped they didn't dent Dom and Evie's car.

I walked to the side door of the apartment building and opened it, catching a sudden whiff of cooking meat. My stomach growled. Poor Rufus was probably salivating upstairs with all the good smells wafting up the hallway.

I took Rufus downstairs and to the fence post, where he always did his first pee of our walks. As I stood there, a loud bang from the house startled me.

The front door was open. I couldn't see inside, but I could hear the slams of something — or someone — getting beat up. I pulled Rufus back toward the front door and peered inside.

A broad-shouldered man had a sledge hammer and was pounding away at something on the floor. He slammed the head of the hammer into a brown cabinet, spraying wood everywhere. The landlord, with a frown, was standing out of the way of the sledge hammer. The broad-shouldered man was laughing.

He was drunk.

The landlord saw me, and the man swung again, then stopped when he saw me.

"Everything okay?" I asked.

"Yeah! We're taking out this old record player. Got to make room for the new TV!"

"Oh." It was in four jagged pieces on the floor already, easy enough to take outside. "Okay, then."

Rufus tugged me back out onto the lawn.

What to wear, what to wear.

Should I go Goth with all black? Or wear a t-shirt and jeans?

Decisions, decisions.

I decided on a red t-shirt with blue jeans. I took Rufus out for one more walk, and then sat outside.

Downstairs had blown up into a full-fledged party that bled out into the backyard. Cars were in the driveway and up and down the street. The smell of spicy food came through the open windows, and it was loud enough to drown out the TV. They played Spanish dance music and seemed to be having a grand time. I stayed upstairs.

At around eight, it died down, but when I went downstairs at nine to wait for my ride, the lights were still on in the apartment and there were still cars in the driveway.

A two-door blue car pulled up.

"Hey," Scott called from the passenger side. He got out and pushed the seat forward for me to get in the back.

I crammed into the back seat, which was just like being in Evie and Dom's Camry.

I glanced at Tyler through the rearview mirror. "Do you know where this place is?" I asked.

"Sure," Tyler said, though I didn't think he sounded very convincing.

I scooted over to sit directly behind Scott.

"We were there on Wednesday. It wasn't busy."

"But this is Friday," I said. "They're probably going to be really busy."

I crossed my arms and sat in the back seat as we headed back into downtown Providence.

We drove around the northern part of downtown for a while, looking for a parking spot. I suppose I could have helped with that, but I wasn't in the mood. We finally found one, in front of a red-bricked church.

Scott held the seat down for me as I climbed out. I put my hand on his waist and pulled him into a hug. I glanced at Tyler. I wanted him to see me with his ex, to know that his ex was mine.

Tyler was looking down at his keys, then looked across the street. "We're about two blocks away," he said.

Scott pulled away and locked the door. "That's not too bad," he said.

We walked the two blocks. There were other bars with lines of people outside of them, bouncers at the doors, checking IDs. "I thought you said they weren't checking IDs."

"They didn't on Wednesday," said Scott, as Tyler got in line.

I took Scott's hand. He tried to pull away, but I said, "Trust me." As they were looking at Tyler's ID, I cast the "Unsee Me" spell, and Scott and I walked past the bouncers, who looked at us but didn't see us. We went in, following Tyler.

The place was dimly lit. I could barely see Tyler's back in front of me. I was still holding Scott's hand, not because of the spell, but because I liked holding his hand. Tyler waded through the bottleneck at the door, and headed into the club proper.

In here, it was just as dimly lit, with dark corners, and blinking colored lights on the dance floor. It was probably like any other bar, except there were only men dancing with men. I kept my eye on Tyler, until a stunningly beautiful blond woman walked in front of me and distracted me. I knew it was a man under that red miniskirt, and he winked at me. I turned away. Scott stayed close to me, however.

"Lost Tyler," I yelled at him over the music.

"Let's go upstairs," he yelled back at me, and this time he took the lead, pulling me toward a set of metal stairs that led to a second floor.

There were more dark corners here, men standing or sitting, making out or doing other things that I had to tear my eyes away from. Men were holding men, hugging them. I put my arm around Scott's shoulders and pulled him to me. He sighed, I don't know from relaxation or pleasure. We stood at the railing. We swayed to the music, dancing our own beat upstairs.

I felt free here. Free enough to nuzzle Scott's red hair. He made a noise that only I could hear. It was different than at home. Here, here I could show my feelings for him out in public, without fear, without getting dirty looks. My hand wandered down to his waist and I pulled him closer.

He sighed again. Then my phone vibrated in the pocket that was pressed against him.

He chuckled and pulled away as I tucked my hand in my pocket. I took it out and looked at the number on the tiny screen. It was Becky's number. I answered it.

"Hello?"

"Mike! They were here! In my house!"

"Did you call the police?"

"Yes, they're on their way. Mike …"

"Okay, when you're done with them, I want you to come to the apartment."

"Are you —"

"Just do it."

"Okay," she said. I hung up and looked at Scott. "We have to find Tyler."

"Who had to call the police?"

"Becky. They broke into her house."

"Oh, no." Scott looked out onto the dance floor. "We'll never be able to pick him out of this crowd."

I could light up the place with a bright light, like I had done the night we were attacked.

"Do you have anything of his?"

Scott shook his head.

"I'll go check the bathroom."

"No!" Scott sounded frantic for a minute. Then he calmed down. "I'll check it."

I could have checked the bathroom, but I don't know why he didn't want me to. Maybe he didn't want me to get into a fight with Tyler, since I would physically drag him out of a stall if I had to.

We went back downstairs, to a dark corridor crowded with men. Scott threaded his way through to a door and went inside. Men kept examining me, but I gave them a look I had perfected in prison to make them go away. Just as I thought Scott had been swallowed by the bathroom leviathan, he came out the door.

"Not there," he said. He took out his phone and started calling someone. "I can't get any reception in here."

"We'll leave."

We went to the main doors. The bouncers stared at us. "How did you two get in here?"

"Sorry," said Scott, and we bolted out the door.

We got out onto the sidewalk. Scott tried calling again. "He's not answering his phone."

"Dammit," I said. "What if we go to the car?"

He nodded. "I'll keep trying."

We walked the two blocks back to the car. As we turned the corner, I saw Belial, in his black armor and fiery eyes, standing by dark lamp post. "Use me," he said. "I can find your wayward man."

Scott stopped when I did. "What's wrong?"

"Do you see him?"

Scott looked in the direction I did. "See who?"

"Do you even *sense* him?"

Scott then looked at me, back to the lamp post, then back to me. "Mike, are you okay?"

It was like Grimalkin. Only I could see him. I took Scott's hand again and stormed past Belial, who only laughed at me.

"Mike, what did you see?"

"Nothing. Nothing. Never mind, a trick of the light."

We kept walking, and we got to the red-bricked church we had parked in front of.

Except the car wasn't there.

SIX

THE REAL ME

S COTT AND I STARED AT EACH OTHER, then at the spot where a small yellow tricked-out truck sat. Scott whipped out the phone and tried again.

"Come on, answer the damn phone!"

"I'll kill him."

"No, Mike. He must've had a good reason for this."

I crossed my arms.

As I gazed at Scott, a police car drove by us slowly. It stopped right in front of the truck.

"You boys lost?" asked the policeman in the passenger's side.

"Our ride left us," Scott said.

I had learned to let Scott do the talking. People seemed to be calm and easy around him, and to believe him. I put on the defenses, giving short, curt answers to questions. I was definitely not comfortable around cops. I shoved my hands in my pockets and tried to look innocent.

The cop looked at me. I wondered what was going through his mind. I was afraid he would arrest us for being together.

"Where you from?" he asked Scott.

"Thayer Street."

"If you hustle, you can probably catch the last bus."

"Okay, thanks," said Scott with a smile.

With one last glance at me, the cops drove away.

"Where's the bus station from here?" I asked.

"That way." He pointed vaguely north. "Maybe we should run for it."

I nodded, and we both broke out into a jog. Scott said he jogged around his neighborhood, and I did too, as well as jogged on the treadmill. However, when we got to a brightly lit but empty Kennedy Plaza, we were still winded.

As we paused to catch our breath, I found the Hope Street bus parking spot and looked at its schedule under plastic. I could barely see the times, but I thought I saw one at 10:48. It was 10:45 right now, according to my phone.

We were okay by the time the bus arrived. It opened its doors, but no one came out. We waited, climbed aboard. The bus driver looked tired and bored.

We paid our fare and sat down toward the back. "When Tyler comes back to your place," I said, "punch him in the face for me."

"You know I can't do that," Scott said with a small sigh.

"Then call me and I'll do it."

"I'll ask him why he did it first."

I snorted. The bus stopped and picked up three kids, all younger than us. They wore jeans and t-shirts, and each had a red bandanna on their person. *Obviously a gang,* I thought.

They sat at the back of the bus, a bit away from us. I watched them warily, while Scott sat up straighter. We went through the College Hill tunnel, and I half-expected them to attack then. But they didn't.

Scott got off at his stop. "I'll call you later," he said to me.

As he rose, the guys in the back got up too. I got up, ready to follow if they were going to go after Scott. But he disembarked alone.

However, the guys in the back moved closer to me. One of them sat next to me. As the bus moved, I felt something sharp against my side. It was either a shiv or a knife.

I turned my body and looked at him. He was grinning at me. With my left hand, I grabbed his hand with the knife, squeezing. He yelped in pain. All the fury of the night gave me strength. I moved my right hand to his head, and pointed it down toward the floor. His body followed, and he fell off the bench. I put my foot on his neck as I still held his hand.

I glanced at his friends. They were just staring, not moving.

I looked down at the kid. "We cool?" I asked, pressing ever so slightly on his neck with my foot.

"We're cool, man."

I let go of his hand, removed my foot and let him scramble up. They probably thought that since I was alone, and my clothes were new, that I had money. They left me alone, but I still wanted to be sure they wouldn't follow me. So I waited until the stop after my house to get off.

I watched the bus turn the corner to downtown Pawtucket, then started walking back to the apartment. When I got there, I could see on the curb, the pieces of the cabinet — which had actually been a phonograph — lay on the curb. The silver car was still there, and the first floor had all its lights on.

As soon as I hit the second floor, I took a breath of sweltering hot air. I wished I knew where the air conditioners were, and so I could put them in. Rufus was panting.

"I know, buddy," I said, and took down his leash. "We're going to wait for Becky downstairs."

As we waited, some people left the apartment downstairs. One was that broad-shouldered man, along with Jason and another woman. Rufus barked at them. I pat the dog, reassuring him.

Jason and the woman hugged the house, while the man, who I assumed was Jason's father, reached out and let Rufus smell his hand.

"Nice dog."

Rufus gave it a whiff and settled down.

The man patted his head. "What's his name?"

"Rufus," I said.

"Good dog," he said, and smiled at me. "See you later."

"See you."

The lights in the downstairs apartment started going out right about then, and I found myself in darkness with Rufus. I was starting to come down from the adrenaline rush with the panic of being stranded, and the short-lived fight with the kid. I closed my eyes for just a minute.

"Mike, is that you?"

I opened my eyes when Rufus' tail hit me because he was wagging it so hard. I stood up and stretched.

"Yeah, Becky. It's hot as hell upstairs."

She stepped into the yard, closing the gate behind her. She had her suitcase again.

I handed the leash to her while I took the suitcase. "Is it me or is this heavier than the last time?"

"My books are in there. I have to study for a test."

I hauled the suitcase upstairs, and we went into the heat. I turned on the fans, which helped a little.

"Sorry, it's hot up here."

"It's safe," she said.

"Do they know who did it?"

"I do," she said. She looked at me. "Can we talk about it tomorrow? I'm bushed."

"Sure. I'm tired too." I gave her a quick kiss. "See, I didn't unmake the couch. It's ready and waiting for you."

She chuckled, an involuntary noise, and then her face crumpled. She started to cry.

I went over to her and held her. "It's okay," I said, rubbing her back.

"I'm so sorry, Mike. I don't know what to do ..."

"We'll take care of it."

She pulled away, looking like a wreck. "You smell like a bar."

I laughed. "I'm too tired for a shower."

I got her a napkin from the counter. She smiled, wiped her face and blew her nose. She parted from me and tossed the napkin in the trash.

"I'm going to bed," I said. "I won't come out until morning."

The next morning, Saturday, I was up early. It had cooled down overnight enough for a light blanket. I passed by the couch on my way to the bathroom. Becky was sound asleep.

I took Rufus out for his walk and when I returned, Becky was still asleep. I didn't bother being quiet while I fed Rufus and started breakfast.

There was a moan from the couch. "What time is it?"

"Seven-thirty."

"It's a Saturday."

"Yes, and?"

She sat up on the couch and looked bleary-eyed at me. "Don't you sleep in?"

"I'm used to getting up early."

She moaned and collapsed back down on the couch.

"Come on and get breakfast."

"Yeah, yeah," she said, and got up, going to the bathroom before sitting down across from me. I had perfected breakfast sandwiches on English muffins, and slid one to her.

"How did you sleep?"

"Not enough." She picked at her sandwich.

I took a bite. "So who broke into your house?"

She sighed. "The Church."

"Why would they do that?"

"To scare me." She took a tiny bite of the sandwich. "They left a Bible on my kitchen table, with passages marking what happens to those who turn away from God."

I took another bite, thinking. What if a demon appeared during the service? That would straighten them all out. It might be worth going back to prison just to see their faces.

No, no, no. Bad Mike.

"Mike, you're thinking about demons, aren't you?"

I felt my face get hot. "Is it that obvious?"

She laid her hand on top of mine. "I don't want you to get in trouble."

I smiled. "It's true. I'd get in big trouble."

"You never told me why you summoned a demon."

"Because I got beat up in middle school, and I wanted to punish them." I finished off my sandwich. "He killed eight people before they banished him."

"Oh, my God." She took her hand off mine to cover her mouth and her eyes went wide.

"Yeah. But I wasn't in trouble for that. I was in trouble for the summoning in the first place."

"Do you … you don't summon demons anymore, do you?"

I sighed. "I'm trying not to."

She squeezed my hand. "You don't need to summon demons. You can take care of anything if you trust in the Lord."

"That's just it, Becky. I don't trust anyone."

"You trust Scott?"

I looked down at her hand. "Eat your breakfast before it gets cold."

"You're avoiding the question."

I moved my hand out from under hers. "I trust him, but if he knew *everything* about me …"

"I think he'd still care for you."

I shook my head. She and Scott didn't need to know that the eight men and boys dead were people I wanted dead and, at the time, I even wanted more. If the Rosicrucians hadn't caught Belial, the whole town would have been murdered. I noticed that I could still carry a grudge. This was something I needed to deal with.

She took the breakfast sandwich and tossed it out. "I'm not hungry anyway." She looked at the coffee maker. "Can I make some coffee, though?"

"If you know how. That kind of technological alchemy is beyond me."

She laughed, and hugged me across the shoulders.

"I'm going to go to the library, then to Scott's store. Will you be all right by yourself?"

"I have Rufus." She smiled at the dog, who wagged his tail. "Besides, I have to study."

"Okay. I have my phone."

Jessica didn't work in the library on Saturdays, but Lillian did. I didn't get her a coffee. The library usually had half-days on Saturdays, closing at noon. I checked my "mail", but nothing was there. I picked out a book on Egyptian history and sat down. I didn't read it, but I sat and thought.

I could go to the service at Becky's church and I could disrupt it with a little bit of magic, more flash than substance. Put halos on people, brighten the area around me, make sparkles dance around the minister or priest or whatever he was called. Or I could make it seem like the place was on fire but nothing was consumed. Or I could set the Bible the minister might be reading from on fire.

I smiled as I let my imagination run away with me. What could I do that would still stay within the terms of my parole but would scare the bejesus out of them?

Anything using my own will. And there were a lot of things I could do.

I heard a sound near me. I opened the book to look like I was reading, just in case Ritter decided to drop by. But he didn't, and my imagination took off again.

I left the library at eleven because I started going down darker paths. What if I could somehow entice someone into punching someone else, and then a fight breaks out, and … Yeah. I needed a clearer head.

Scott's store was open and a couple of women were inside, looking through a basket full of stones.

Scott nodded to me. "Hey."

"Hey," I said. "Where's Tyler?"

"Hadn't come home when I left."

"Maybe he knows better."

"I'm worried. He's not answering his phone still."

"Do you think I had anything to do with it?"

He blinked. "No, why would I think that?"

I know I blushed. "Oh, nothing."

"Mike, did you do a spell?"

The women stopped and turned to look at us. I hunched my shoulders and again tried to look innocent. I don't do a very good job at that. It makes me look even more guilty.

"What did you do?" Scott asked me, his arms crossed and giving me one of those accusatory glares that most mothers are famous for.

I withered under his gaze. "It was just — just to get him to leave."

He looked away from me. He seemed to be disappointed. I walked toward him. "Scott, I —"

"If he's hurt, it's on *your* hands," he said firmly.

The two women stood close to each other, looking from me to Scott and back again. They looked like they didn't want to be there.

"He's not hurt," I said, though how the Universe wanted to work the spell, it could mean that he *was* hurt. He wasn't dead. I threw him in the trash. "Maybe he went somewhere."

Just then, I saw Tyler pass by the window, strutting like he had just gotten laid. He stepped into the store and grinned at me and Scott.

"Where have you been?" demanded Scott. "I've been calling you."

"I lost my phone," he said, still grinning. "But I found this really hot guy in the bar."

"You left us there," I said, turning to him. I wanted to slap that grin off his face.

"You seem to be fine," Tyler said, looking me up and down, dismissing me. He walked past me over to Scott. "I lost you in the bar. But this guy —"

"You didn't even try to look for us. We were right upstairs, looking for you. We had to take a bus back."

The door bells tinkled as the two women left the store. Scott sighed. Tyler said, "I was going to ask if I could get my things. I'm going to be staying with Ralph for a little while, until his boyfriend comes home."

"And then you'll leave?" I asked.

Tyler turned around to me. "Is that what you want?"

"Yes."

He turned to Scott. "Do you let him tell you what you want?"

Scott said, "I'll go to the apartment so you can get your stuff." He looked beyond Tyler to me. "Can you watch the store until I get back?"

"Sure," I said.

Scott stepped out from behind the counter and I took his place. Tyler followed Scott out the door and started talking to him as they walked away, toward the parking garage.

I was alone. "Grimalkin," I called.

Nothing happened. He didn't appear.

"Grimalkin," I said again, putting more force into it.

Was he afraid, now that Belial had appeared to me those few times?

"Grimalkin?" I dared not say *I summon thee*, because that would break my parole. And I didn't want to call Belial.

I closed my eyes and pictured Grimalkin in my mind. Black skin, horns, cloven hooves.

"Grimalkin," I called, and pushed that picture out.

I opened my eyes and he appeared before me. But he wasn't as solid as usual. I could see the posters on the wall through him.

"Grimalkin —"

He raised a hand. He said, "Too protected."

Of course. Scott performed healings here, so he would have protected the place.

"Should I go to the service?"

"Why?"

"To scare them."

"This is not your fight."

"They are hurting someone I care about."

"Do you love her?"

I shrugged. "Like cousins." He tilted his head. "Like family."

"Tell Knights."

What could the Rosicrucians do about it? The church was a Christian group, most likely, and the Rosicrucians went after people who were the opposite.

"Ask them first."

I had the business card to the Atheneum in my wallet. It was still early, even if Scott came back. I pulled out the card and, according to the business hours, it wasn't open on Saturday. But there was a phone number on the bottom.

Scott had a phone in the business, so I used it and called the number. Grimalkin disappeared the minute someone picked up.

"Yes, Grimaulkin?" said that old man's voice.

"How did you know it was me?"

"Just a feeling. What is wrong?"

"I want to ask a question."

"Go ahead."

"My cousin is being harassed by a church."

He paused. "You mean a cult."

"Maybe. I don't know."

"You want to go find out."

Well, I wanted to do more than that, but I answered, "Yes."

"You're asking permission?"

"If they are a cult, can you do anything about it?"

"Yes, we can do some things about it. They are perverting God's Word."

I thought about maybe becoming a Knight, if that meant I could go after these guys. But then I'd have to be all holier-than-thou, and I wasn't ready for that. I'd have to be like Ritter. No, thank you.

"So can I check them out?"

"Yes. When are you going?"

"Tomorrow, I think."

"Report to me at the library on Monday."

"Okay. Hey, um …" I turned the card over in my hand. "I didn't catch your name."

"No," he said. "You didn't."

He was silent while I waited. "Okay, then. I'll see you Monday."

"Indeed."

I hung up. Next, I called home. The answering machine picked up. "Becky? Becky, it's Mike. Pick up."

I heard her pick up and got the feedback screech in my ear. "Hey, Becky, is there any way you can bring me to the church?"

She gasped. "You want to go?"

"I need to scope out the enemy before I do anything to them."

"Mike, are you sure?"

"Sure, I'm sure."

"I have to work tomorrow, so we'll have to leave right after the service. They usually have a get-together for lunch afterward, but I have to drive from Worcester …"

"You can leave me at your apartment. I'll clean up while you go to work."

"I don't have any clothes for church."

"Then we'll go to your apartment on the way."

She said, "What are you going to do?"

Scott walked in and his door bells tinkled at his entrance. "Nothing, I swear. I promise on Scout's Honor to be a good boy."

She giggled. "You were a Scout?"

"No, but I can still promise on my honor."

"Okay. Okay, we'll have to leave early."

"No big deal."

"When are you coming home?"

"A couple more hours," I said, winking at Scott as he walked over to me. Scott's poker face didn't change. "Two or three."

"All right. I'm going to make lunch, then."

"Okay. I'll see you soon." I hung up and smiled at Scott.

Nope, didn't change.

"Scott —"

"You cast a spell to get him to go away."

"I thought you wanted him to go away."

"Gods," he said. "Not to be forced."

"Doesn't sound like he was forced."

"He didn't stop talking about this Ralph guy the entire time." Scott rolled his eyes. "What am I going to do with you?"

I moved out from behind the counter and walked up to him, putting my hands on his waist. "Kiss me?"

He sighed, but he smiled. Then he did kiss me.

SEVEN

TAKE ME TO CHURCH

B ECKY LOOKED SO PLAIN in a short-sleeved long yellow dress. It had no gatherings, no fit. It just looked like a sheet with a hole in the top for the head and sleeves, and it was straight to the floor all the way down. She wore white flat shoes. I got away with a polo shirt and khakis — my usual "dress-up clothes".

We were at Becky's apartment. It was bigger than Dom and Evie's, still a one-bedroom, but with a separate kitchen and living room. Both had looked tossed, the furniture tipped over, books torn out of their shelves, a glass snowglobe lay unshattered near the TV, which sat on the carpet, screen down. The only place untouched was the kitchen table, on which was a Bible with colored tabs sticking out of the side and top. While Becky got dressed, I read some of the tabs. They talked about how God was a jealous God and didn't want anything else coming between Him and "His people".

I believed that it was more of an It than a He. I had invoked demons in His name. Of course, *something* existed.

Becky came out, looking sheepish when I smiled at her. "That's your Sunday Best?"

"It's not what we look like in the sight of men, but our hearts in the sight of God."

"Are you serious?"

"Mike, if you say that while we're there, they're going to preach to you."

"You make that sound bad."

"It is, Mike. If the preacher corners you, he'll preach and use you."

"That's not bad. It's just words."

She shook her head. "He does something. He makes you feel guilty, feel unworthy, and the next thing you know, you're being baptized."

I laughed. "I summon demons. I already am unworthy."

She drove there in relative silence, steeling herself up for something. I suppose when the kids saw her last time, they would have told the church. She was probably getting her story straight.

We got off the highway and ended up driving down a rutted dirt road that seemed to lead into an open field. We drove over a hill and saw parking, row upon row of cars, and a large tent. Next to the tent was the frame of a huge building, bigger than the tent, easily two stories high and as wide as the entire lot that my apartment building took up.

"What's that building?" I asked.

"The Tabernacle. Where they plan on doing their preaching, worldwide."

"Pretentious, aren't they?"

"Tower of Babel," she said quietly, as she parked the car where someone wearing a bright yellow construction vest directed her.

We got out of the car. She locked it and put the keys in her purse. She stood up straight. I walked to the front of the car, and offered her my arm. She smiled, and threaded her arm through mine.

As we walked into the tent, I saw TV cameras in the back of the tent. I raised an eyebrow at that.

Becky took a spot in the back, toward the middle of a rough-hewn bench. Most people crowded as much as they could toward the front. A young girl sat next to Becky, but no one sat next to me. Becky scooted away from her, her hip hitting mine. I glanced around Becky to the girl and made a magical motion for her to leave.

She looked around for a minute, confused, and then she got up. Becky exhaled. She whispered, "Thanks, Mike. She was a plant."

"A plant?"

"To watch me."

I had to do that three more times before the service actually started. First, at the front of the tent, a group of boys and girls filed in, their hands together in prayer, holding books between their hands. Then a bunch of people in suits or modest dresses came in and sat down at the front row.

The people in the tent rose as the boys and girls started singing a hymn. I had no idea what song they were singing, but Becky did, and she mouthed the words without singing.

Then there was a reading from the Bible, the King James version. I could tell by the language — it was colloquial.

More singing. More readings. More singing. More readings.

It got boring. I tried to pay attention, but it started getting really hot under the tent, and I wanted to sit down.

A man got up from the front row and started speaking about the readings that had just been read. He explained the importance of the Word of God and other things that I honestly forgot. Then two other people got up and spoke.

The woman was a little spitfire, nearly yelling into the microphone, sweat dripping from her, and she looked like a screaming harpy. I couldn't understand what she was saying toward the end, but she put the microphone back and sat down, as if proud of herself.

Then a man, probably in his 30's, got up. He wore a suit like the rest of them, but the first thing he did when he got up to the podium was loosen his tie and unbutton his top button.

"Please, brothers and sisters, sit down."

He seemed pretty well-built under that suit. He had very short brown hair, a round face and, from what I could see, seemed to have something that made me want to pay attention to him.

"I see some new faces here. I welcome you to the Waters of Life church. As you can see, right now, we're in the midst of building a more permanent structure. But with the help of God, we will have a new building to celebrate our love of God and his only Son."

He spoke about the construction, how the building was going to be used, then he talked about the school that was going to get built along with it, and then the day care, and how precious and important the young were ... I drifted off to open-eyed sleep.

Slam!

"Wake up!"

Everyone in the room jumped and sat up straight.

"Wake up and listen to the Word of the Lord! Is this the time to sleep? The Lord's light is here, in this room, among you! And the evil, the dark, is in your heart!"

He spoke with pure passion. I looked at Becky and her eyes were wide.

He said, "When Our Lord saw the man possessed, the Lord cried out to him and called him Legion! In the name of the Lord, he cleansed this man, and sent the demons into pigs, and the man was cured! He was cleansed, in the name of God, by the power of God."

He looked toward the rear of the tent, over the heads of everyone seated there, his eyes like a searchlight. He was looking for someone.

"Come unto me, Legion, and I can cleanse you of the demons in your soul."

He said this so quietly, so calmly, that I wasn't sure he even said it. I found myself hunching down low in my seat, trying to hide.

He's talking to me. He's talking directly to me.

His eyes found us: the two of us, sitting in the back, alone.

"The Sabbath Day is for what?" he asked.

"Rest," someone said.

"Worship," said another.

"The Lord!"

He nodded. "Yes, yes, yes. Is it for work?"

"No!" responded the crowd.

"Is it for pleasure?"

"No!"

"It is for the Lord! And yes, it is for us, for us to come together as a community, as a family."

"Amen!" someone yelled.

"Amen!" the crowd yelled back.

I looked at Becky. She was shaking. I reached over and took her hand. His eyes left us, and moved to someone else. "Do you covet?"

"No," a few people said.

"Liar!" He slammed his palm down on the open Bible in front of him. "Everyone covets! Everyone wants something. You come here to worship the Lord. You want the Lord to bless you. You want the Lord to notice you. 'Bless me, oh, Lord, for I have sinned.' The Lord won't bless you if you demand it. If you come here expecting Him to notice you. You, the special you — different, more holy than the rest, more pious. 'Notice me, oh, Lord.'"

A few people looked down.

"You're NOT more holy. You're NOT more pious. God can see through you. He can see your heart, how black as coal it is. How prideful you are …"

He went through the Seven Deadly sins, one at a time, looking at different people as he spoke, as if he could read their hearts. Women burst into tears under his gaze. Men swallowed their own emotions and looked like beaten children.

"But listen." He cupped a hand to his ear. "Listen," he whispered. "Do you hear the Word of the Lord?"

"Yes!" someone cried out.

"Do you hear that the Lord loves you? The Lord loves you, all of you, even *you*." He looked beyond everyone to us again. "Do not turn away from the call of the Lord." He looked at everyone. "The Lord cares about you. He cares about your life. He wants to see you happy, not struggling. And you are struggling. You are turning from the One who can help you. But you struggle against him, wrestle against his angels."

He continued, "The angels sing when you return to him. The angels will be beside you forever if you come to the Lord. Listen, harken, harken to his Word. Let us pray."

Everyone got up and the choir started to sing a psalm. The preacher came down from his pulpit and walked up to people, speaking to them individually, holding their hands, or touching their foreheads, and they would cry out in a loud voice, or fall backwards. It got crazy. Songs bled into another song, as the preacher worked his way through the crowd.

He broke his way through the crowd and he came striding toward us. He came alone. We were rooted to the spot. I still held Becky's hand.

He stopped in front of Becky. He looked down, reached down and took our joined hands. "Rebecca. We love you." His hands were warm, dry and firm. He had some power there, lying beneath the warmth. Like he could shoot lightning bolts from his palms.

She let go of my hand and started to cry. "But I have to work."

I took my hand back. I didn't like the connection.

"If you come back to us, we will make you safe."

"I need to work. I need to go to school. Please, Pastor, I can't stop now."

"The Lord will provide. He provides the sparrows with food in winter. He can help you, if you return to us."

"I have to go to work."

He patted her hand. "Your mother and father miss you. Please come back."

She tore her hand from his and put her head in her hands. She was really crying now.

He turned to me. "Legion," he said. "I call you Legion."

I said nothing, but I made a protective motion. He reached down and covered my left hand with his right. I felt the power pour into me, like Scott's. But while Scott's was a lazy river, his was a waterfall, shoving its way into my aura.

"I can cleanse you in the Lord's name. Use your magic for good."

I opened my mouth to say "No", but no words came out. I stretched my senses to look for Grimalkin, but I didn't sense him there. I didn't dare look for Belial.

"Summon the angels, not the demons. Shimael. Gabriel. *Michael*."

I gulped. What if I could control the angels? The real angels, not the fallen angels.

"You can see God and the wonders of Heaven, Michael. I can banish those demons back to hell, and you can be free."

The people in the front of the room had turned around to see the preacher with us.

"Free to be with her," he looked pointedly at Becky.

I blinked. The spell was broken. I narrowed my eyes. "I don't covet any woman."

He stared at me, and then his eyes widened as he realized what I said.

I removed my hand from his, and took Becky's arm. "Let's go, Becky."

"You struggle against God's Will!" the preacher called.

I turned my back to him. Becky slipped between the benches, and out into the aisle, toward the TV cameras. They had all been trained on us the entire time, and then they turned from us to follow the preacher again, though one camera followed us out.

"I'm sorry, Mikey." She sniffled.

"Don't be," I said, putting my arm around her shoulders. I glanced back at the tent. I half-expected her mother to come running out. Or her father. But it didn't happen.

We walked back to the car. Alone together.

I finally blurted out, as we were on I-495, "He's got some power."

She knew who I was talking about. "He said he was touched by an angel when he was a boy."

"Angels." I snorted. "More like fallen angels, if you ask me."

"How do you know?"

"Because angels don't concern themselves with men unless God tells them to." I watched the scenery pass by. "And God doesn't care."

"Oh, Mikey, God cares."

"God didn't summon that demon, I did." I thumped my chest. "Me. If God didn't want that demon to come into existence, he wouldn't have let me summon it. Besides, while I was in that holy prison, there were plenty of chances for God to come along and tell me how saved I could be."

"Don't be angry at God."

"I'm not angry at God. I just don't need him."

Becky sighed. "You know, my old self would argue with you. But some days, I think you're right. That God has left us all to take care of ourselves. Preachers are there keep us in line. But after it's all said and done, God isn't going to care if I worked on His Sabbath day or not."

"Because you're living a good life, Becky. A *human* life."

She glanced at me and smiled, then turned back to the road. "You are too, Mike."

"I'm trying like hell."

We got back to her place, with just enough time for her to change into her work clothes and run back out the door. "I should be home around 9:30 and then I'll take you home," she said.

I surveyed the living room after she left. It really wasn't that bad, once you moved the large items back to their respective places. The TV cable had been yanked out of the back of it, but otherwise it was fine. I picked up the snowglobe. It said "Montreal, Quebec" on it.

I remembered for a minute when we went to Montreal. I must have been very young, 8 or 9. I remember it being boring, going in and out of shops, driving around the city, looking at uninteresting buildings. My mother went into a fancy boutique, and the lady there fussed all over me. I remember Phil being rambunctious, hiding among the racks of clothes. My father ending up taking us kids outside for ice cream.

Phil. I wondered what he'd be doing right now if I hadn't killed him. Well, *I* hadn't killed him; Belial had. Under my orders, but I really didn't kill him, did I? Just like the seven other people.

I had five years to think on that, and decided that yes, I had killed them all. Maybe the Rosicrucians knew and set me free because they figured I felt remorse. But oftentimes, I didn't. I was glad Phil was gone, because I always felt he was in my way. Even now, with my father, his specter was in the way.

I placed the snowglobe on the entertainment center, above the TV. Just as I did, the phone rang.

She must have had an answering machine, I thought. But it didn't pick up after the fourth ring, so I did. "Hello?"

"Who's this?" said a woman's voice.

"Who's *this?*" I replied back.

"Becky's mother."

About damn time, I thought. "Aunt Sue, it's Mikey, Maggie's son."

"Mikey? I thought you ran away."

"I did, but I came back."

"Praise the Lord, the Lord Jesus led you back to us."

"Uh, no."

"Angels protected you. Your mother must be so happy now."

"She was," I said.

"I know the love of a mother can almost equal the love of the Lord Jesus for us. Jesus' love helped you to survive."

"No," I said. "Anyway, why —"

"Why do you say that? You were probably out on the streets, sinning so greatly, and now the Lord has brought you back."

"No, Auntie Sue. I was in prison."

"What for?"

"Summoning demons."

She gasped. "Pastor Greene said that you were possessed, Mikey. You need to come back to us right now, so Pastor Greene can put you right."

"No, I don't think so."

"Mikey, it's *awful* to be possessed by demons. You don't have any control —"

"It's not awful, and I do have control. I know what I'm doing."

"The demons are already in your mind."

I said nothing. She was right about that; I didn't want to be rid of them. Where would my power come from, then?

"We can cleanse them from your soul."

"No," I said. "I think I'm all right." Then I hung up.

She called again. It rang a good twenty times before she gave up.

By the time Becky came back, I had done the living room and was working on the kitchen, threading a drawer onto its slider.

"I'll bring you home," she said.

She looked bushed. If I didn't have Rufus to worry about, I would have told her I would crash here. But Rufus hadn't been out all day. I got the drawer on the slider as she came out of the bathroom.

"You sure you're okay to drive?"

"Can I stay another night at your place?"

"Of course."

She drove with the windows down, to try and stay awake. It was a 40-minute drive, but it seemed longer. We got to the apartment around eleven, and Rufus was waiting at the door, his tail wagging furiously.

He was a good boy and had waited the entire time, piddling only in the bathroom. We had a very short walk and when I got back to the apartment, Becky was already sleeping.

EIGHT

I LET BECKY SLEEP AS I GOT READY TO GO TO THE ATHENEUM. I left Becky a note telling her to call me when she got up.

It was already warm as I started walking to the bus stop. I noticed an unusual car on the street: a black Town Car. I walked past it, and heard doors open. Turning around, I saw two men get out of the car and head toward me.

I didn't know either one. They were both in button-down short-sleeved shirts, looking like bouncers to me. One slipped something onto his hand. Brass knuckles, glinting in the early morning daylight.

I smiled. "Good morning, gentlemen."

They said nothing but kept walking toward me. I stood my ground, whispering a spell to keep me from getting knocked down. I wouldn't be rooted to the spot, but I would not go down.

"What's this all about?"

"Maybe your girlfriend won't like you much after you get your face bashed in," said the guy with the brass knuckles. I saw the iron rod in the other man's hand, and knew these guys were playing for keeps.

I assumed a ready stance, standing straight, hands up, palms open. The guy with the rod swung at me, and I deflected it, but I wasn't able to deflect the brass knuckles that came at me. He connected with my shoulder, my bad shoulder, unfortunately, and pain exploded from there, filling my vision with red.

My right arm went down, not to come back up again. I turned my body to the right, and Iron Rod hit me in the back this time.

Magic would be necessary at about this time. "Feuer!" I yelled, and gathered what consciousness I could, throwing it into a fireball in my hand, which I threw at Iron Rod.

He screamed, his clothes catching fire. Brass Knuckles either didn't see it or ignored it, as he slammed his fist into my temple.

I stumbled, but didn't go down. Pain cried out behind my eyes. The magical fire that caught on Iron Rod disappeared. My will was dispersed. I was dizzy and confused.

Iron Rod swore at me and looked around for his weapon. I heard someone yell, "Hey!"

The two men turned around and through my clouded vision I could see a heavyset man coming our way. He yelled at us, "What the hell you doin'?"

"C'mon, let's get outta here," said Brass Knuckles, heading back to the car. But the man was between them and the car. I wouldn't be surprised if they were going to beat him too.

"Hold!" I yelled at them, and pushed with my will. I clenched my hands into fists.

They stopped moving, frozen in place. The heavyset man stopped moving too, more mystified that these guys weren't coming for him.

The cops showed up right about then. It helped that we lived right down the street from the high school, and there were cops there every morning dealing with kids who wanted to start their early mornings with a fight or two.

The two men only turned their heads. Brass Knuckles still had his weapon on. I released my hands, and the two men stumbled forward as the cops approached them.

"What's going on?" asked one of the cops.

"These guys were beatin' up that kid," said the heavyset man. "My wife called you."

One of the cops had looked down at Brass Knuckles' fist. He immediately grabbed him and turned him around to face the nearest car, placing his hands on the roof. The other cop did the same to Iron Rod. They were frisked while I leaned against a short wooden fence, trying to see clearly and get my bearings back.

The heavyset guy came up to me. "You need an ambulance?"

"No!" I said. I still owed money from my last visit to the hospital.

The cops found guns on both of the guys.

"I got a permit for that," said Iron Rod when they pulled the gun out from his jacket.

"Uh huh," said the cop, putting wrist cuffs on Iron Rod.

"He used that," I said, and pointed to the iron rod on the ground.

"How can you still be standing?" asked the second cop who had Brass Knuckles and was leading him to the car.

"Luck and skill," I said. I could focus on the cops now.

Another police car arrived, and Iron Rod was led to the second vehicle. The cops held a little conference in the road.

The cop who spoke to me came up to me. "Do you need an ambulance?"

"No," I said, a little calmer.

He retrieved the iron rod I had pointed out. One of the other cops was talking to the heavyset man.

"What's your name?" asked the cop with the Iron Rod. The vehicle Brass Knuckles got shoved into left the scene.

"Mike LeBonte."

"Do you have an ID?"

"No."

"You sure you don't need an ambulance?"

"I'm sure."

"Mind if I go look you up?"

"Sure," I said. He went back to the car and called it in. I wondered if it said I had been in prison. The other cop joined him soon after.

I smiled at the heavyset guy. "Thanks," I said to him.

"No problem. I gotta get to work. You take it easy, okay, kid?"

"Yes, sir," I said.

Both cops came back to me. Neither of them looked kind or gentle.

"What were you in prison for?" asked the one who hadn't talked to me yet.

"I would have thought it said."

"It said, 'Other'."

I sighed. "Summoning demons."

The cops looked at each other, then back to me. "That's a crime?"

"In magical circles."

"This is Hotch and Fernie's department," he said.

"Detective Hotchkiss? I've worked with him."

They both seemed to breathe easier. "Tell us what happened."

I told them what happened from my point of view.

One walked back to the car, while the other asked, "Any old enemies from prison coming after you?"

"No, but someone I'm helping just got robbed." I told them about Becky's apartment getting broken into.

"One of the detectives will be calling you." I gave them my cellular phone number. He nodded as he took it down. "Probably not Hotchkiss, though. It's not weird enough for him."

They left, and I continued to the bus stop. People stared at me. It wasn't until I saw myself reflected in the window of the bus that I saw why.

The side of my head was swollen and my eyes were wide, the pupils dilated. Did I have a concussion?

I walked to the Atheneum. The sunlight outside was starting to give me a headache. I tried the door and it opened, even though the hours didn't say they were open.

The cop was at my left. I showed him the business card. He nodded. "Please take a seat over there." He pointed to a high-backed chair to my right, in the corner, lit by a dim Tiffany lamp. I went and sat down, and the cop plucked a phone handle from the table beside him.

He dialed a number and murmured something in the mouthpiece. I tried to listen, but didn't dare use magic here. He placed the receiver back down, and said, "He'll be right with you."

About ten minutes later, I saw the Knight in the gray suit come out of the shadowy depths of the library. He wore a black shirt this time.

"Please come with me, Grimaulkin."

I got up and followed him to the back of the library.

"Do you drink coffee?"

"No. It sucked in prison."

"Tea, then?"

"I trust that."

He went to his chair and turned around to look at me. On the table beside him was a teacup with what looked like brown tinted milk. On the table beside me was tea with just enough milk to give it a little color. In it would be, most likely, three sugars.

"What happened to you?"

"I got in a fight this morning."

"You have a concussion." He approached me. "Let me take a look at it."

I gave him a little nod, and he hobbled around my chair to the back of it. I felt him put his hands on either side of me, but not touch me. The right side hurt suddenly.

"Ow." I tilted my head to the left and hit his hand.

"Hold still."

Then I felt coolness, similar to Scott's river of cool water that could fill me. I felt the throbbing ease, and noted the room got a little darker.

With Scott, I would close my eyes and let his cool water wash over my shoulder, which is what Scott had concentrated on healing over the last couple of months. I didn't want to close my eyes. I didn't trust this Knight.

"Relax, Grimaulkin."

"What are you going to do?"

"Heal you."

I snorted. Scott was a healer. This kind of felt the same. The cool water filled my mind, and I found my eyes closing, relaxing. The water fell down to my shoulder, and seemed to quench the fire of pain there. It went to my ribs, filled my torso and lungs, and I took a deep breath. It felt like clean mountain air, not a dark, musty library.

I heard him hobble away and I snapped my eyes open so that he wouldn't catch me in a relaxed pose.

He didn't look at me, but went to his chair and sat down. "Feel better?"

I rolled my shoulder. "Yeah."

"Good. Now, tell me what happened at the church."

I told him about the service. "Then when he touched me, I felt some power there."

"In him or coming out of him?"

"Drawing from me. He called me Legion."

The Knight sat up straight. "You do know what that means, don't you?"

I swallowed, looked away.

"Do you hear voices, Grimaulkin?"

He sounded genuinely concerned. I didn't look at him.

"Grimaulkin, if you were possessed, we would have known it by now."

"I'm not possessed. I know what I'm doing." I finally looked at him.

He almost whispered, "Do you hear voices?"

We stared at each other. He tried to read me, to sense my uppermost thoughts, but there was nothing there. Grimalkin wasn't there, Belial wasn't there. No one rushed to my defense. What could I say?

"What if I do?"

"Are they telling you to kill people?"

"No, of course not."

"What about harming yourself?"

"No. Look, I don't know what this has to do with anything. These people are harassing my cousin. She's trying to make a life for herself and she can't —"

"Do you see things others can't see?"

I thought for a moment of Belial, that I could see him and Scott didn't see him. And as soon as I thought it, the Knight sat back, making a steeple of his fingers, pressing them to his lips. I tried to not think of it, but you know when someone tells you not to think of an elephant? All you can think of is the elephant.

"You went to the Confessor in the prison," he said.

The Confessor was sort of like a psychiatrist, that they would bring you if you started acting strangely. Ritter kept bringing me to the Confessor way more often than others.

Ritter would catch me in meditation or staring at the wall, or talking to myself. So off to the Confessor, where I would spend an uncomfortable half-hour saying I was praying.

"You never told him about this." He brought his hands down to the arms of the chair.

"No. It was none of his business." *It's not your business, either.*

"Grimaulkin," he said calmly. "You took that name in prison. There is no demon or angel in the any of the grimoires named Grimaulkin. No spirit anywhere by that name."

I needed to change the subject. "How did we end up talking about me? Are you going to help me or not?"

He followed my thread, and we got away from talking about myself. "What if we don't? What will you do?"

"Help my cousin get out of that church."

"How?"

I was thinking of casting some sort of spell to block them from bothering her, but that would also mean her mother and father would be blocked. I'd have to ask her permission before doing such a thing. I searched my mind for something proper to say to him.

But he caught my thought. "Where would you get this spell? You don't have any grimoires, do you?"

"Isn't that against my parole?"

"It's not if you own them, but only if you use them with other entities. You are not allowed to summon entities. That means angels, demons, or spirits. I'm sure they told you that much."

"Yeah, they did," I said with a frown. "I don't have any grimoires."

"Just the voices in your mind."

That's when I did the old spell that Grimalkin taught me in the prison, so that even the Confessor couldn't get into my thoughts. I envisioned a solid vault at the front of my mind, and the door just shut. He would sense nothing now from me.

The Knight looked steadily at me. He was pushing against my mind, I know he was.

I asked, "So are you going to do anything about the Waters of Life?"

"We will research them."

I got up. He watched me stand.

"What will you do?" he asked me.

"My own research."

"Be careful, Grimaulkin. We don't know anything about them yet." He used his cane to help himself stand.

"Right," I said. This was a waste of my time. They weren't going to do anything. I would have to take care of this myself.

As I walked to Kennedy Plaza I called the apartment. I said through the answering machine, "Becky, it's me."

She picked up. "Hey, Mike."

"Anybody call?"

"No. Are you expecting someone?"

"No, not really. Are you working tonight?"

"I'll have to leave here at noon. I'll stay at my own apartment tonight."

"You feel okay with that?"

"I have to deal with this."

"When are you working next?"

"Wednesday."

"Okay. If you don't feel safe, come over. But Dom and Evie will be back next week." Which meant I had to take care of this by then.

"All right, I will."

"I have the key, so lock the door when you leave."

"All right. I'll call you if anything weird happens."

If I could, I would send an entity, a servitor to watch her. But that was a definite no-no. I told her goodbye and hung up the phone.

I arrived at Kennedy Plaza. A man in ragged clothes walked up to people, handing out little booklets and saying, "Jesus loves you." He caught my eye, and, at first, started walking up to me.

I made a motion, a threat. Don't come near me. He stopped in his tracks. Then, his eyes went wide, and he bolted across the street, just missing a moving bus.

That guy was definitely a sensitive. Some people are more sensitive to magic than others. What would be a gentle nudge to most people could be a huge shove to sensitives. Scott was a sensitive, but not like this guy. Scott had created buffers, ways to sense but without being overwhelmed. You couldn't be a healer without being sensitive in a way.

I got on the bus heading to downtown Pawtucket. The bus ride was uneventful and, when I got off, I went right to the library. I could do research on the Waters of Life, too.

I waved hello to Jessica and walked over to the research section.

"Hey, Jane?"

She put down the book she was entering in the computer, turned to me and smiled. "Hi, Mike."

"Hi. I need some help."

"Sure, what can I do for you?"

"I need to research a church that's in Worcester."

"Like how old it is, or what denomination?"

"'Church' might not be the right word."

"Ah," she said. "Is it Christian or something else?"

"Christian."

"Let's use the Internet." She came out from behind the desk.

I never noticed her limp when she walked, like one leg was shorter than the other. She seemed to walk sideways, her entire body shaking when she stepped on her left foot, then she'd swing out her right foot, stand a little taller for a half second. She hobbled over to the bank of computers, where only one person sat at the small desk with a computer on top of it.

She sat down next to him at another desk as I stood over her. She used the mouse and keyboard to get to a website called "Yahoo!"

"What's the name of the group?" she asked.

"Waters of Life."

She typed into a field, "Waters of Life Worcester" and a list came up. "They have a website and everything," she said. She peered a little closer. "And there's some things from the Worcester Telegram Gazette."

"What's that?"

"The local newspaper in Worcester. And the Boston Globe." She got up. "See this? When you hover your mouse over the link, the underlined blue words, it tells you where it's from."

"I didn't know that," I said, watching her do the movement. My interest was piqued by the newspaper articles. I sat down across from the computer.

The Waters of Life was established in 1997. Reverend Edward Greene registered the group as a non-profit church in 1998. They were first a storefront church, looking like they lived hand-to-mouth there. Then, in February of last year, they received a large amount of money all at once. The Boston Globe reported in March they purchased some land outside of Worcester. In May, they moved out of the storefront. The most recent article about them stated that they were building a church for about half a million dollars.

I sat back, thinking. Where were they getting their money from? I went to their website. I found everything I had read, dates for milestones, contact information, and pictures of the Reverend in action. There was a phone number and P.O. Box in Worcester as their address.

I then looked at biographies. I saw the screaming woman, named Laura Pike. I saw Uncle Andy listed there, with a very short biography. It said he had one daughter. I now understood what Becky meant by her parents pretending Danny, their own son, didn't exist.

Reverend Greene was last. He was an ordained Methodist minister, and he "saw a vision" that he had to establish his own church. He started from "humble beginnings" in 1995. He initially predicted that the world was not going to end in the year 2000. The year 2000 would be the beginning of a new way of life.

"He considers himself a healer, a conquerer of disease, all in the name of Jesus Christ," the biography continued. "He has healed many of the congregation who had lost hope. They came to Jesus and were healed of everything from diabetes to inoperable cancer."

The last link was their hours, when and where they had prayer meetings and their Sunday service. I didn't want to drag Becky to a prayer meeting, especially after seeing her reaction at the Sunday meeting. Maybe I could get Frank to help.

I shut off the computer, got up, and stretched. It was already two o'clock, and I hadn't eaten lunch. I said thanks to Jane, and went to the Chinese restaurant. I bought what I could afford (two egg rolls and a small wonton soup) and headed over to Frank's office.

"Come in," called Frank after I knocked on the door.

"Hey, Frank," I said, walking in and sitting down across from him.

He sniffed the air. "Chicken soup?"

"Wonton soup. Close enough, I suppose." I took the container out of the bag.

"So what's up?"

"Find anything new about Becky's suitors?"

"They're the mob, Mike."

I calmly found the spoon in the bag and took it out. Balancing the container on my lap, I took off the lid. "So does that mean you're not going to do anything?"

"I'm just a PI from Maryland. Crossing swords with the mob is putting your life in your hands."

"I'll —" I thought about the two thugs who attacked me earlier that morning. I was going to say I'll take care of it, but I knew they had the drop on me. If I walk into a place where the mafia held court, loaded for bear, I would be dead in minutes.

"You'll what?"

"I'll talk to them. Do you know who I need to see?"

"I'd start with Herb Carabesi."

I spooned out a wonton and bit into it. "At his office?"

"You sure as hell don't want to show up at the bar he frequents. They'll stop you at the door."

"Do you know it?"

"I might. But hell, Mike, you're tempting fate."

"If I show up at his doorstep, it means I know something about him that he doesn't know I know."

"If you show up, they could kill you and dump your body in the river."

I sipped the soup, drinking it from the container. "I promise to be a good boy."

Frank shook his head. "I won't tell you the bar he goes to."

"Then can you bring me to his office?"

Frank sighed. "As long as you don't ask for the red Corvette."

"Let me call to make sure he's there."

"Do you remember the number?"

"Of course." I picked up Frank's rotary-dial phone. *Grimalkin*, I called in my mind. *What's the phone number to Herb Carabesi's Cadillac?*

He told me, and I dialed it. A pleasant-sounding woman answered the phone. "Hello," I said. "Is Herb Carabesi there?"

"Who's calling, please?"

"Someone he tried getting in contact with early this morning."

"One moment, please."

I listened to some tape-recorded music that sounded muddy. "What happened this morning?" asked Frank.

I held up my hand. "Tell you in a minute."

The woman came back on. "Hello, sir. I can make an appointment."

"How about four?"

"Four o'clock today?"

"Yes."

"Three p.m. is his last appointment."

"Three p.m. is fine." I'd have to inhale my lunch. "We'll be there in a few minutes."

Frank waited until I hung up before he said, "So what happened?"

"Two guys attacked me."

"Why didn't you tell me?"

I put the lid back on the soup. "Because I'm okay. I took care of them. They were arrested."

"And were probably out in two hours. You're crazy, Mike."

"That's why you're going to wait for me outside."

He gathered his keys. "I'm just as crazy."

His office was enclosed one-way glass, up at the top of a set of glass stairs at his car dealership. The receptionist was pretty for a woman, but way too made-up for my taste. She pointed up the stairs.

I knocked on the door.

"Yeah," said a voice, not Carabesi.

The door opened from the inside and a big goon stood there. He stepped aside a little to let me in.

He started to frisk me. I automatically raised my hands. I was used to this from prison. Across from me was Mr. Carabesi, sitting at his desk. The room smelled of old cigarettes.

"You're the kid from the wedding."

"Yes," I said.

When the goon stopped touching me, I stepped forward, again, a habit from prison. The goon grabbed my shoulder and hauled me back, so I was a few feet away from Carabesi but within arm's length of the guy.

"Whaddaya want?"

"I want you to leave my cousin alone."

He raised an eyebrow. "Cousin?"

"The cute little blond girl who lives in Franklin."

"You two goin' out?"

"No. She's my cousin."

"Who's her boyfriend?"

I sighed. "She doesn't have one."

"What're you involved for?"

"Because you're scaring her. She doesn't want to go out with you or any of your guys."

He pulled out a pack of cigarettes. He waved with his hand, and the guy behind me let go of my shoulder. He offered the pack to me. I shook my head.

"Good. Tryin' ta quit." He put the pack aside. "What did you do to my guy, settin' him on fire?"

"Magic," I said. "Illusion. It wasn't real fire."

"And you did somethin' to hold 'em still for the cops."

"Yes."

"Magic?"

"Yes."

He leaned forward. "What else can you do?"

I shrugged.

"Can you do real fire?"

"No." That would require an entity. No summoning, remember?

"What if you do some work for me? I can leave your cousin alone."

"Work for you? Mr. Carabesi, I know what group you're involved with. I'm on parole."

"I can pay off any parole officer."

"Not these guys. They're magicians, too."

The goon behind me said, "I don't believe this kid."

Carabesi said with a nod, "I don't believe him, either. But you got some nerve coming in here and telling me to stop going after your cousin." He picked up the pack again. "What'll you do if I don't?"

"I'll do more than freeze your men in place for the cops to come."

He laughed.

I wanted so badly to do something. To lift the desk, to set the pack of cigarettes on fire in his hand, to throw the phone at his head. Belial whispered a spell in my mind, and I smiled.

"Okay, then," I said. I turned around and opened the door. The goon was laughing too.

I stepped on the first step, and said the spell. As soon as I was on the next step, the glass step behind me shattered, and fell down next to the receptionist. She screamed and ran from her desk. I took each step, each one shattering behind me as I walked down the stairs. I got to the bottom of the stairs, and saw the goon in the open door, looking down at the remains of the steps.

I walked to the front door of the dealership. I raised my arms, gathered my will and yelled, "Harm none. Shatter!"

When I brought my arms down, every piece of glass shattered in their frames, a loud chink echoing through the showroom. I turned and opened the front door. That's when the glass fell out of the door to land in pieces at my feet. It started a chain reaction — glass in the cars, glass in the showroom windows, glass surrounding the second floor office, glass on the picture frames, all came down like fine diamond rain. People ran covering their heads, but the glass bounced off them, not hurting them.

The last bit of glass tinkled down from the second floor, while everyone on the floor of the showroom slowly rose from their ducked position. I walked through the shattered glass doors to Frank's car.

Frank said to me as I got in the car, "What the hell was that?"

I put on the seatbelt.

"War."

NINE

CRAZY (NOT)

FRANK LECTURED ME ALL THE WAY HOME, using expletives I hadn't heard since prison. I was too busy planning my next move to pay attention. Should I contact the Knight at the Atheneum? Will Ritter come after me?

"You can drop me off at home," I said to Frank while he stewed at a stoplight.

"You'd better sleep with a gun, Mike."

"Are you still going to help my cousin?"

"Yes, of course I will. But I don't want to scrape you off the sidewalk after someone guns you down."

He pulled in front of the apartment. "Thanks, Frank."

"You going to see Scott tomorrow?"

"I plan on it." I undid my seatbelt and put my hand on the door handle.

"Wait there for me."

I paused. "Um, okay." I turned to look at him.

"Just do it. Now get out of my car."

"Right." I got out and he took off, heading toward downtown Pawtucket.

I went into the house. It was still hot as hell, and Rufus was waiting at the door. I grabbed the leash and took him out.

I took the phone out of my pocket, flipped it open, and dialed the Knight's number. It rang three times, and I almost hung up, but he picked up.

"Yes, Grimaulkin."

"I did magic in public."

"The gas leak in North Providence?"

"What gas leak?"

"It's all over the news. An explosion at a car lot."

"I didn't explode anything. No one got hurt."

"Which is a good thing for you because Ritter would be right behind you."

I turned around. No one. Whew.

"Tomorrow, you will go to the car lot, apologize to the owner, and ask what reparations you can make."

"He's a wise guy."

He paused. "Be careful, then." He hung up.

I stared at the phone. I flipped it closed, muttering, "That was no help."

I called Scott.

"Hey," he said. I could hear him smiling.

"Lonely?" I asked.

"Peaceful, thank you," he said with a chuckle. "Are you okay?"

"Why shouldn't I be?"

"You didn't call me for a couple of days."

"Been busy. Can I ask a favor?"

"Where do you need a ride to?"

I laughed. "You a mind-reader now?"

"Whenever you ask me for a favor, it usually means a ride."

"Tomorrow morning."

"Before I open the store?"

"Yeah. Around nine."

"All right. Where to?"

"North Providence."

"You know there was a gas leak there? Blew up a car dealership. They closed off Mineral Spring Avenue."

"That's where we're going."

He said quietly, "Mike, you didn't …"

"I did."

"Oh, God. Did anyone die?"

"No. I made sure no one got hurt."

"Why did you do it?"

"The manager pissed me off."

"Were you trying to buy a car?"

"No. It was the guy who went after my cousin at the wedding."

"Your cousin is complicated," Scott said. He paused for a minute, as if waiting for me to contradict. I couldn't. "I'll pick you up tomorrow, okay?"

"Okay."

As Rufus dragged me back to the apartment, I thought about what Scott said. *Your cousin is complicated.*

Was it for a reason?

I didn't want to go upstairs. I went over to the cellar door, Rufus standing at the foot of the stairs to the second floor.

"Stay there," I said, and tried the door to the cellar. Locked. No big deal. I spelled it open.

I found the light switch on the wall, and it lit the bare bulb that shined its light to the base of the stairs. I walked down and went over to where I had found the air conditioners. My shadow was swallowed up by the darkness in the deeper reaches of the cellar.

I saw a small thin chain above my head, and tugged on it. Another bare bulb highlighted the area I stood in. Just beyond was a wire cage with a padlock on it. There was no light over there. I had to tilt my body to see what was in the wire cage.

It looked like some model cars, other toys, plastic bins, and a table covered by a wool blanket. I didn't think that this belonged to the landlord. I spelled open the padlock. The floor was dusty, except around the table covered by the blanket. I lifted the blanket and found not a table, but two air conditioners stacked one on top of the other.

"Thank God," I whispered. I folded the blanket and set it on top of one of the plastic bins. I lifted one of the air conditioners and climbed the stairs with it to the first floor. I set it down at the bottom of the stairs leading up to the second floor. Rufus sniffed it as I went upstairs, unlocked the door, and threw it open.

Rufus dashed upstairs, and I unhooked the leash. Whenever I did that, he knew he was getting a treat, so he sat calmly, waiting. Instead, I went downstairs and got the air conditioner. I set it on the kitchen counter, then went back down to the cellar to get the second air conditioner. By the time I got upstairs the second time, I was sweating from the heat. Even though the air conditioners were light, compared to what I usually lifted, they were awkward and it was damn hot.

I put the second air conditioner on the coffee table. Rufus stayed in the kitchen, waiting patiently for his treat.

"Good boy," I said, shutting the door. I gave him two treats.

After putting one air conditioner in the living room and the other in the bedroom, I stood in front of the one in the living room, drinking in the cool air. The phone rang, but I was too comfortable to move. I let the answering machine pick up.

"Hi, Mike, it's Becky."

I hung my head and turned toward the phone.

"Everything's okay. Just letting you know. Okay. Later!"

The answering machine beeped when she hung up.

"Finally," I said to Rufus. He grinned at me.

I fed him, ate dinner, yawned a lot, and went to bed in a much cooler bedroom.

I walked out of the house with my gym bag over my shoulder into a cloudy day. When I got to the end of the walkway, I saw Ritter leaning against a black sedan, his arms crossed as he gazed in my direction.

"About time," he said. He opened the passenger side door. "Get in."

"Why?"

"You have an apology to make."

"You're not here to arrest me?"

"No." He nodded toward the car.

Slowly, I walked to the car and climbed in. Ritter shut the door and walked around the front, then got in the driver's side.

"Seat belt," he ordered, and I put it on.

"Do you know where it is?"

"Yes," he said, pulling out of the parking spot.

"I didn't summon anything to do it, you know."

"I know."

This was going to be a silent, uncomfortable ride.

I asked, "Can I put on the radio?"

"No."

"You're mad."

He looked away from me, checking traffic.

"I know you're mad. You were my guard for five years. I know you too well."

"Grimaulkin, if it were up to me, I would put you in a hole for the rest of your life. You're unsafe."

"Unsafe? Really? Come on, Ritter."

"You lied to us."

"When?"

"You saw things in prison. You never told us." He took a right turn onto Mineral Spring Avenue. "You would have gotten out earlier if you had."

"What?" I stared at him.

"You know there's no magic in that prison. We have protections, runes and sigils to eliminate any magic. I knew you saw something. We could have gotten you help."

"What do you mean?"

The traffic was stop-and-go up the road. He turned to look at me. "You think you're possessed?"

I know I blushed, because I felt my face get hot.

"By who?"

"You wouldn't know."

The light turned green and he proceeded down the hill. "You took the demon's name? There's no such name as Grimaulkin. There is a word grimalkin, which is an old female cat, or the name of the witches' cat in Macbeth. How did you know this name?"

"He told me."

"You saw this demon in prison."

"Do we need to talk about this?"

"Yes. This changes things."

"How?"

"Did you see this demon in prison?"

"Geez. Yes."

"What does he look like?"

"A goat-footed demon. Black skin, black hair, black ram's horns. No tail. Naked."

He snorted. "Of course."

"What? I can't see anything. He's hairy down there."

"I suppose that your imagination can fill in the details."

"Do we really need to talk about this?"

We were at the set of lights just before the car dealership.

"You're in luck," Ritter said. "Now we get to talk about your apology."

"I just say I'm sorry." We pulled into the parking lot. There was plywood enclosing the showroom now. "I don't even know if the guy is here."

"He's here," Ritter said, putting the car into park behind a white Cadillac with an HERB1 license plate. "Come on."

He got out of the car. I did too. I crossed the front of the Cadillac, while Ritter met me at the doors. He opened the door and let me in.

The cavernous showroom echoed our footsteps as we walked in, crunching glass in some places. I heard someone coming, and turned in that direction.

Carabesi came out from the waiting room of the service area. He stopped short when he saw me. Then he looked up at Ritter. "You this punk's father?"

"No," Ritter said, straight up, while I almost burst out laughing.

"You see what he did? And to my cars? My goddamn office!" He pointed at the exposed office above.

Ritter looked at me. I took a step toward Carabesi. "I'm sorry."

He backed up one step. "Sorry? That all you can say, is you're sorry?"

"Is there anything I can do to — to help clean up?"

"Do you have any idea how much money it's going to cost for me to fix this place?"

"I can help with that," I said.

Carabesi crossed his arms. "How?"

"Drum up business."

"In this condition? I have to shut down for at least a week for them to do all the repairs!"

"I'll get people in. Run an ad, saying that it's a construction sale, and put in the ad a symbol I can give you. It'll draw people in."

"Is this magic?"

"Yes."

Carabesi looked at Ritter. I glanced at Ritter myself. Stone-faced as ever.

"You can only use it in that one ad," I cautioned. I would have to put a time limit on that sigil or everyone in the state would be coming to his dealership forever. "Got a pen and paper?"

"Yeah, come over here."

He went back to the service center. Even there, the glass had shattered. The goon from yesterday was there, and he jumped up from his stool. He glared at me, and thrust his hand somewhere inside his jacket.

"It's okay," said Carabesi. "He's gonna pay for the damages." Carabesi rummaged under the counter and came up with a blue pen and plain white paper.

I closed my eyes for a minute. I don't know who burned the sigil into my mind's eye, but it appeared like they always do. A little more complicated because I had the time limit, I started to draw the sigil on the paper, starting from the middle.

When I finished, I handed it over to him. It looked a little bit like Celtic knotwork, a complicated swirly pattern in a compact space.

"Put this on the ad somewhere within the next week. Make sure that a person can pass their eyes over it. Don't put it in the corner. Hide it in the black of the ad."

He took it from me, turned it around in his hands.

"I'd also suggest you have every single salesman you've hired available. It'll bring people in, but it won't sell the cars for you."

Carabesi studied it, tilting his head. "You sure this'll work?"

"You doubt me?"

"I don't believe in this magic crap." He looked at the plywood on the wall behind him. "But I guess ..."

"Can't hurt, right? What's the worst thing that could happen?"

He shrugged. "If it works, then we're okay. If it doesn't, you still owe me, kid." He looked up at Ritter.

"Understood," said Ritter.

He tapped my arm above my elbow, and I automatically walked in front of him, like I used to do in prison when I had to go to my cell. I didn't look behind me, as I had been trained. I walked until he told me to stop.

We got to the car, and he said, "Get in."

I got in, the gym bag between my feet. I put on the seatbelt and he backed out of the parking spot.

"Can you bring me to the gym?" I asked.

"Yes."

I looked out the window. My hopes that he wouldn't go back and talk about Grimalkin were dashed.

"You used to talk to that demon," Ritter said. "I used to see you do it."

I sighed.

"Yes, we really need to talk about this. Because this changes everything. We can stop the voices."

"I don't want an exorcism."

"You're not possessed. I would know. You would be dead."

"All right, then, how can you stop the voices?"

"Medicine."

I turned to stare at him. "Medicine?"

"Medicine and psychotherapy. Honest psychotherapy."

"What, you think I'm crazy?" I crossed my arms.

"If you had admitted to this in prison, we could have given you the treatment you need."

"I'm not crazy."

"I never said you were crazy. I said you were unsafe."

"Because I see demons and I hear voices?" Okay, so that did sound crazy. I had to change the subject before I thought about it. "Do you know where the gym is?"

"Yes. We can make this part of your parole —"

"I don't want any medicine. Or psychotherapy." I looked out the window again.

"Don't force us to do this."

I gazed out the window. We were silent for a long time. The whole time he drove into downtown Pawtucket, I thought, I'm not crazy.

He stopped in front of the YMCA. I got out of the car without saying good bye or even a thank you.

I worked out harder than I usually did, to get out the thought of me being crazy.

Psychotherapy. Really? I don't need that. They can't see the demons because they're part of my will, like Belial said. They attached themselves to me like a leech. In return, they would tell me spells. It was a fine arrangement. So what if I talked to myself sometimes.

I wasn't crazy.

I was drenched in sweat when I got off the treadmill. I had run a mile, the most I had ever run in one time. I planned on going for a long swim, hard enough to make my arms hurt.

Max entered the room. "Hey, man," he said.

"Hey," I replied.

"You okay?"

I tilted my head side to side. "Got pissed. Working it off."

"You should meditate." He smiled at me.

I said, "You know, that's a good idea."

I went back to the locker room, took a shower, and changed. I found an empty office with the door open. I went inside.

There was only a desk with an old dial phone on it, and a small desk chair. There was nothing on the desk, so I sat on it. I closed my eyes, took a couple of deep breaths, letting thoughts flow past me.

"So they think you're schizophrenic."

I opened my eyes to see Belial in his armor, his fiery eyes through his helmet.

"You had to tell them," he said. "You had to admit that you saw Grimalkin. Now they will try to banish us both."

"I never admitted I see you. Then they'll think I'm possessed."

"You know what they will do. They'll force you to take the medicine and we will go away. All your spells, all your power. Gone." He snapped his fingers. Even though he wore armored gloves, I heard the snap.

"I know that." I didn't want that to happen. "They can't force me to take the medicine."

"You should make sure of that."

"How?"

"Use your computer."

Belial knew what a computer was? That was weird.

I knew that I was going to have to take a side trip to the library.

Belial disappeared. I jumped down off the desk, grabbed my bag, and headed across the street.

⊗　　⊗　　⊗

"Oh, Jane, my most wonderful friend in the world."

Jane laughed as she turned from her computer to look at me. "Flatterer. What do you need now?"

I had put together the question on the way over. "Let's say my brother is crazy. Can I force him to take medicine and go to a psychiatrist?"

She pursed her lips. "'Crazy' how?"

I decided to use the word that Belial had used. "Schizophrenic."

"Paranoid schizophrenic?"

"I don't know. I guess?"

"I can't answer a hypothetical without all the information, Mike." She got up. "But let's take a look at some sources."

It took about a half an hour of perusing big, thick, green books with the state seal embossed in gold on them. She finally found what she was looking for. "There's three types of commitment into a hospital or a mental institution."

"Okay ..."

"The first is involuntary commitment. That's if you're found by a doctor to be harmful to yourself or others. The second is voluntary commitment. You allow yourself to be admitted to the hospital because you think you'll harm yourself or others. The third is observation. You stay overnight to make sure you're safe."

"So only a doctor has to say I'm insane?"

She jerked her head up and stared at me for a second. I didn't even realize I had said "I" until she stared at me. I smiled.

She looked down at the book. "You have to bring 'your brother' to the emergency room, and then they decide if he'll harm himself or others and need to be kept for at least observation. Is he a minor?"

"No," I said, thankful yet again that I was at the magic age of 18.

"It's harder to involuntary commit adults."

I relaxed. First they'd have to drag me kicking and screaming into the hospital, and then I would lie my way out of it. Easy.

I squeezed Jane's shoulder. "Thank you."

She smiled. "I hope this eases 'your brother's' mind."

"I'm sure it will."

I left the library, feeling much better. I went down the hill to Scott's store.

Scott was busy rearranging the herbs. Frank was sitting on the folding chair at the end of the counter.

"Where the hell have you been?"

"How pleasant to see you, too."

I walked up to Scott and planted a kiss on his cheek. He smiled at me.

"You were supposed to call me," Scott said.

"I already took care of what I needed to do." I nodded to Frank. "I gave him what he wanted."

"What's that?" asked Frank.

"Money. Or the chance to make money."

"You gave him one of those things like you gave me?"

"I gave him something to place in his ad for this weekend."

"Why can't you give me something like that?"

"Do you have big display ads in the newspaper?"

Scott chuckled.

I stepped away from Scott and asked Frank, "So what did you want me to come here for?"

"I'm going to take you to the range and show you how to shoot a gun."

I know the blood ran from my face. "No, Frank, I don't need that."

"Magic won't save your ass when someone's coming at you with a gun."

"Neither will a gun," said Scott. "I agree with Mike."

I rubbed my shoulder. "You should know how I feel about guns."

"You can't be afraid of them," said Frank.

"I took care of the guys, and I took care of Carabesi. I'm fine."

"What about your cousin?"

I had forgotten all about her in the heat of the moment. "I'm sure Carabesi will leave her alone now that he knows what I can do."

"I suggest we do a drive-by, just to make sure."

"She called me last night. She said she was fine."

"You scared the crap out of him yesterday. That doesn't mean he won't stop stalking her today."

I looked at Scott. "But I wanted to spend tonight with Scott."

Scott leaned against me for a moment. "Don't worry, Mike. I'll be around."

Frank got up. "You and the dog are coming with me." He stormed to the door. "Three o'clock, be here."

"Okay."

Frank walked out. I smiled at Scott. "Alone," I said. "Finally."

Scott chuckled and blushed. I turned to him and put my arms over his shoulders. He leaned against me, gripped my arms. "I've missed you."

"Me too," I said, nuzzling his hair, kissing the top of his head. I loved the smell of him. "You sure you want me to go with Frank?"

"It's your cousin. It's for a sense of completion, to make sure that everything's all right with her."

I hugged him tight. "Maybe we can close the store."

He laughed. "I only close it for a healing or a reading. Not for quickies."

"I'll make it worth your while." My hands moved downward.

He gasped. "Mike …"

"I'll go lock the door."

"No, Mike. Please?" He turned around in my arms and faced me. He put his hands on my chest. I took a deep breath of him, and leaned forward for a kiss.

He kissed me, long and deep, like I really wanted as a prelude to something more. When he pulled away, I gasped for air and fought to keep myself down.

I didn't succeed.

"Did you ever have to arrest someone who was crazy?" I asked Frank, as we went up I-95 north to I-495.

"A few times."

"What did you do?"

"Put them in handcuffs and drove them to the hospital."

"Did they stay there?"

He shrugged. "I don't know. We always had to fill out a special form for them."

"What happened that you got fired?"

"A drunk driver got me pissed off. I physically threw him in the car. He was a state representative's brother-in-law." He turned onto 495. "Shit rolls downhill, Mike. Remember that."

Rufus's front paws were on my lap, his head out the window. I held his collar in one hand and his leash in the other. He would sometimes tuck his head inside, give me a sloppy kiss, and then stick his head out again.

We got to Becky's house, and her car was in the driveway. We drove around the block and parked the car up near the beginning of the street. We had a good line of sight to the front of her house.

I had been on these watches before with Frank. Most of the time it was watching a house to see who was arriving, who was leaving, where they were going. We were told to move along by the cops only once.

Rufus started getting antsy about half an hour in. Frank said, "Ok, go see your cousin. Take the dog."

I left the car, let Rufus take a healthy piss on someone's fencepost, and walked down the street to Becky's apartment house. A car drove by: silver, not black. I was on pins and needles. My senses were tingling, I didn't know why.

I got to her house without incident, and saw a doorbell with her name above it. I rang it.

A little while later, she came downstairs. "What're you doing here, Mike?"

"Checking on you. We wanted to make sure you were okay."

She looked out of the doorway. "Where's your PI friend?"

"Watching for any cars."

She bent down and scratched Rufus behind the ears. "I don't know, maybe he stopped coming after me."

I still felt something weird. I looked out into the street when I saw a car go by. Blue or black, but a small car, not a sedan.

She touched my arm and I jumped. She asked, "Are you okay?"

"Something doesn't feel right."

"Do you want to come inside?"

I shook my head. "No. No." This sense of something bad was really getting to me.

"Okay. I'll see you later?"

"Sure." I left her at the door, and walked back to Frank's car.

I got up to the car. I opened the passenger side door and saw Frank lying unconscious across the passenger side seat.

TEN

PANIC

I SHOOK FRANK, BUT HE DIDN'T RESPOND. I panicked. I ran back to Becky's house, dragging Rufus behind me.

I pounded on her doorbell. When she came to the door, I yelled at her, "Call an ambulance!"

She didn't ask why but dashed back upstairs.

I bolted back to the car and opened Frank's side of the car. "Frank, Frank!" I got a moan out of him.

"Frank. Frank, c'mon, man!" Did he have a heart attack? I wasn't a doctor!

I could hear sirens, far away.

I looked up through the passenger side door and saw someone coming toward me. The house we parked in front of was all lit up, and people were gathered at the doorway.

A slender man in just a pair of jeans and barefoot peered in. "Oh, my God."

"I had someone call the ambulance," I said.

Sirens. Closer now. I turned in the direction they came from. A police car roared down the hill, through the stop sign at the beginning of the street, and parked right in front of us.

"You called 911?" asked the cop as he got out of the car.

"My cousin did," I said. I looked down at Frank. "I just left him for a minute." I pulled Rufus away from the car and let the police peer in.

They hauled Frank to a sitting position. One of the cops opened Frank's shirt, and pulled out a necklace. I couldn't see it, but by then, the ambulance arrived with a fire truck right behind it.

"Diabetic," said the cop, as the paramedics nodded came out of the ambulance. They swarmed over him, and I couldn't see what was happening. I stood at the trunk, listening to them call his name. I could hear Frank moan. Becky arrived, dressed in sweats and flip-flops. She put her arm around my shoulders.

I heard the paramedic ask him, "Think you can stand up, Frank?"

"Uh huh," I heard Frank say.

I watched as he got out of the car, leaning heavily on the paramedic to stand up.

"Let's get you to the gurney," said the paramedic, guiding him to the gurney outside of the ambulance. "When was the last time you ate, Frank?"

"I don't know."

The cop came up to me. "What were you doing out here?"

I told the cop that we were on a stake-out. Becky reaffirmed it.

The ambulance took off. I gave the cop my name, Frank's name, my address and everything else.

"We're taking him to Milford if you want to go there."

I nodded. I looked at Becky.

"I know where it is, but I can't stay. I have class in the morning."

"You can drive me there."

"How are you going to get back here to get his car?"

I stared at the car. "I … I don't know how to drive."

"It's easy."

"Sure it is." I peered in, and saw that he had left the keys in the ignition. How was I going to drive with a dog in the car? "I can't leave Rufus in the car."

"I'll keep him. I'll get my extra key and you can come back when you get out of the hospital and get him. Follow me to Milford." She took the leash from me and walked back to the house.

I panicked again. I had never driven a car in my life.

I carefully climbed into the driver's seat. I put my seatbelt on. That much I knew how to do.

"I don't know what I'm doing," I said, praying for Grimalkin or Belial. I turned the key. Nothing happened. I turned it a little more. It started up. I put my foot on the gas. I remember seeing Scott using that pedal when I would watch him drive the truck. The car didn't move, but the engine revved up.

I scratched my head. I played with the arms sticking out of the wheel column, and found the windshield wipers and headlights. Becky pulled out of her driveway and drove up to me.

"I don't know how to make the car move," I called when she rolled down her window.

"Put your foot on the brake and move the shifter. Move it to D."

"The brake," I said, and had to look down to see where the brake was. I used my left foot, saw the shifter by my right hand, and pushed it down all the way to D.

The car jerked forward. I took my foot off the brake, and the car moved slowly forward. I got to the end of the street and slammed on the brake with my left foot. My body jumped forward, right foot pressing the gas, the car revved. I pulled my foot off the brake. The car shot forward, I turned the wheel, and the car turned.

I was able to negotiate around the block. Becky met me at the intersection of her street. I almost hit her.

I knew for certain I was going to have a heart attack while we crawled down back roads. I gripped the wheel so hard that, really, my entire hand was white. I gasped for air and paid attention to people coming at me. I moved over when I saw someone coming at me. I got used to the brake and the gas eventually.

I had to stop at a red light, in front of a busy street. This street had four lanes, and when she took a left-hand turn, she went into the far right lane. I did the same thing.

It felt like I drove a tank. The steering was stiff, the car was jerky, and I was scared as hell. We only had to ride through two intersections before she pulled into a parking lot.

I had to look for a parking spot. "Please, give me an easy spot to get into."

There was one spot that was extra wide. I decided to go for it. I turned the wheel and pulled into the spot, right in the middle.

I pushed the shifter all the way up to P, which I assumed meant "Park". I turned the key twice backward, and the car's engine stopped. I tugged on the key and yanked it out of the ignition. I rolled up the windows.

Becky waited behind the car. "You look like you saw a ghost." She held up a key on a lanyard. "Just leave this on the kitchen table when you leave," she said.

"I don't ever want to do that again," I said, running a hand through my hair. "How can you drive?"

She laughed. "It gets better with practice. Call me and let me know how he is."

"Okay. Thanks."

She blew me a kiss and drove off.

I looked at how I parked, and realized that I had taken up two spots.

I walked through the big double doors that slid open for me. The crowded waiting room stank of piss, vomit, and sickness. I waited behind a woman with a bouncing, crying baby on her hip, while she explained in a strange accent I didn't understand clearly that there was something wrong with her baby. If I was bouncing like that baby, I would be sick too.

The harried nurse behind the desk said to her, "Go over there, someone will be with you shortly." She pointed to a bank of computers. The woman complied and I came up to the desk.

I gave her a smile and said, "My friend was brought in by ambulance."

"Go down the hall," she said, pointing down the hall in front of her.

I went down the hall to the end, and found myself in the ER. The beds had curtains around them, so I didn't peek inside. Instead, I saw Frank at the end of the row, the curtain pulled aside from his area.

He watched me come down the hall. No one stopped me as I approached. The place seemed like organized chaos, nurses gathered in knots, people dashing hither and yon.

"Hey," I said, as I got within earshot of him. He wore a johnny, a necklace that I had never seen around his neck. It had a red medical sign on it: Mercury's caduceus surrounded by a hexagon.

"Hey," he said. "Pull up a chair." He nodded to the plastic chair next to him.

"What happened?"

"I hadn't eaten anything all day. My sugar dropped. I thought I had candy in the glove box, but I didn't."

"You scared the crap out of me," I said.

He chuckled. "Thanks for calling the ambulance."

"Becky did."

"Did she bring you here?"

"No. I drove your car."

"I thought you can't drive."

"I can't. It was the scariest thing I ever did in my life."

"You didn't crack it up, did you?" Something beeped faster. I looked up at the machine over him, and saw that his heart rate had gone up.

"No. I went really slow. But I took up two parking spots."

"Oh, okay." His heart rate slowed. "We're gonna be here for a while. What's that key around your neck?"

"Becky's house key. Rufus is there."

"Planned for everything, didn't you?"

"Becky thought of it. I wasn't in the right frame of mind."

"See? Magic doesn't help with everything."

"It didn't help me drive." Maybe demons don't drive in Hell.

"I'll take you out to teach you how to drive, if you come with me to the range."

"Frank, c'mon." I sat limply in the chair. Then the doctor came in. He was cute. I mean, really cute. Black hair and blue eyes, clean-shaven, tall and well-built, and in the white coat and scrubs beneath.

"You're his son?" he asked me.

I scoffed.

Frank said, "Oh, hell no."

The doctor smiled. "Sorry. Just an assumption on my part." He turned to Frank. "All right, Mr. Bennett, you know what happened."

"Yes," Frank said, drawing out the word.

"We'll get you something to eat and send you on your way in a couple of hours."

"You can sign me out now and I'll stop at McDonald's."

The doctor gave him a look. "Being that McDonald's is high-fat, high-cholesterol and not healthy for a pig — never mind a human — I can't find it in my Hippocratic Oath to let you do that."

Frank threw his head back on the pillow. "Fine, fine. I'll eat the tuna."

"Turkey sandwich with a fruit cup. That's all we got here."

Frank nodded.

I sat there slack-jawed. He was smart and cute! Who could ask for more?

"Sandy will be in with it in a few minutes. Your sugar was 48, and we need to get it up before letting you go."

"I know the drill."

"Good." He glanced at me, and gave me such a bright smile that set my heart aflutter. "I'll be back in a little bit." He turned and left.

Frank said to me, "Stop drooling. You're embarrassing me."

"Did you see him?"

Frank sighed. "Yes, I saw him."

"Stay here longer. I want to see him again."

Sandy, the nurse, brought a tray with some food and coffee, which Frank said tasted like burnt nuts. I found a bathroom while Frank ate. I saw the doctor again when I came out. He smiled at me. I couldn't tell if it was a come-hither smile or just something friendly.

C'mon, Mike, you have a boyfriend.

Yeah, but I can still look, can't I?

Frank finished eating and, three hours later, they checked his blood, found it satisfactory, and let him go.

I stopped at the desk where the doctor was leaning over and writing something down. I said to him, "Thank you."

He looked up from his paperwork. "You're welcome." He smiled again at me, my heart pitter-pattered, and Frank yelled, "Mike, c'mon."

"We have to go to my cousin's house to pick up the dog."

"It's ten o'clock," Frank said. "Will she be sleeping?"

"No clue."

He found his way back to my cousin's house. As we went down the street, we saw the black sedan in front of her house. He stopped just a little ways before the sedan. I looked at the black car in front of us, looked at Frank, then opened the passenger side door.

I stood on the sidewalk for a minute. I couldn't see anyone inside the car, but I didn't want to take any chances. I gathered my will and began a chant. It would build up a shield around me. Supposedly, according to the wizard who taught me, it would stop bullets. I just had to feel the chant reach its climax, and the shield would be in place.

I walked slowly, feeling the shield form around me, like a light feather touch that actually gave me goosebumps. I got to the corner of the street and felt the shield form a little bit thicker around me, feeling like a heavy coat.

I started up the street. I would pass three houses before I got to Becky's place.

Then the shield felt heavier, and I knew I had gotten to its limit. I ended the chant, walking slower to Becky's house. I watched the sedan. Nobody got out of it.

I rang the doorbell. I thought I heard Rufus bark, like he normally did when someone rang the doorbell. It took Becky a little longer to come downstairs.

She opened the door a crack. Her hair was tousled and she wore a long t-shirt. "You could have let yourself in," she said. She opened the door wider, letting me in while she hid behind the door.

"Were you sleeping?"

"I was," she said. "Is Frank okay?"

"He's okay now." I followed her up the stairs.

She opened the door to her apartment as Rufus stood at the door, his tail wagging like crazy. I pet him as she got the leash from the kitchen table. I took the key off from around my neck and we exchanged leash for lanyard.

"Thanks for watching him for me."

"He was a good boy. We had chicken for supper."

I grasped his head and bent to him. "You got a treat, didn't you?"

He licked me. I chuckled.

"Thanks, Becky."

"No problem."

I let myself out, down the stairs, and outside. I crossed the street right in front of the sedan, and gazed through the windshield.

No one was there.

I let Rufus drag me to the lawn, where he took another piss on a lamp post. I stared at the sedan while he did his business, then Rufus pulled me to Frank's car.

I let Rufus in first, and pulled down my shield. I bent down and touched the concrete sidewalk for the energy to flow out of me and ground myself. If I didn't, I would be all kinds of wound up.

I climbed in.

Then Frank drove through the black sedan.

I looked behind me. The sedan was still there. "Did you see the car?"

"What car?"

"The car you just drove through."

He looked in his rear-view mirror. "I don't see any cars."

I kept looking behind me until he turned right at the end of the street.

"You okay, Mike?"

"Could have sworn there was a car there."

"Did you eat anything today? You could be hallucinating because you're hungry."

"That's probably it," I said. Sure.

Rufus stuck his head out the window for the ride home. I was ready to pass out. I saw that car because I was tired, that was it. Right? Or it could have been some sort of weird psychometry, the sense of seeing something from the past after touching an item from that past. Maybe? Maybe?

I thanked Frank for the ride home.

"Think about going to the range," he said, leaning over on the passenger side seat and looking through the window at me. "It could help."

"I'll think about it, okay?"

Frank nodded, and sat back up. He took off as I stumbled up the walkway, upstairs to the hot-as-hell apartment.

After I put on the air conditioners, I went to the bathroom, then collapsed on the couch.

I dreamed I got a nice French kiss from Scott, when I woke up and realized Rufus was licking my face.

"Ugh!" I spat. "Oh, God, you didn't!" I wiped my mouth and spat again. Rufus sat back, grinning. "You think it's funny, don't you?" I shivered.

I checked the clock after I got out of the bathroom from brushing my teeth and using half a gallon of mouthwash. It was about seven, a little later than I usually woke up.

I got the leash and clicked it on his collar, and we went for a walk. I was being very intensely aware this time around, making sure that no one was going to attack me again. I saw a couple of cars that hadn't been in the high school parking lot before.

I was highly aware that they hadn't been there before. They weren't parked so they could see my apartment house, so I didn't think they had anything to do with the attack.

"I'm getting paranoid now," I said to Rufus as we walked back to the apartment.

I fed Rufus, and planned out my day. No Becky. Nothing going in the library. I could go visit Scott when he opened the store in, oh, three hours. I could go work out again. I could go on the computer.

Or I could do nothing.

In prison, when faced with nothing to do, I either worked out or read. I saw my pile of books from the library, and decided to do some reading.

I read, looking at the clock every half hour or so. I was bored. I put the second book I had picked up aside, and stared at Rufus for a minute. "We'll go outside."

I hooked him up to the leash and brought him out. The cars still sat in the parking lot, but there were other cars with them this time. I walked by them, touching their trunks. They felt real. Again, they weren't parked looking at my apartment.

Feeling a little better, I walked to the woods behind the high school to let Rufus do his business. As I stood waiting, the rear door of the school opened and out walked a guy just a little older than me, in shorts and a t-shirt with a stylized FF in a red circle on it. At the bottom was "Foo Fighters".

"Hey," he said. "What're you doing back here?"

"Bringing my dog out." Rufus kicked backwards as he usually did when he finished taking a dump, and then looked at me as if to say "Ready to go, boss."

"That's not your dog's private bathroom," he said. "You should clean up after it."

"With what?"

"Ever hear of a pooper-scooper?"

"No," I said. I really never heard of such a thing.

"Invest in one," he snapped. He pulled out a pack of cigarettes and tamped down the tobacco.

"What are you doing here?" I asked him.

"Painting." He nodded to Rufus. "What kind of dog is that?"

"A Labrador mix, I think."

"Is he friendly?"

"Yeah."

I brought him over to the guy as he lit up a cigarette. The smell brought me for a moment back to prison, as most of the prisoners picked up the habit instead of lifting weights. No one let me smoke, saying I was too young. They corrupted me in other ways.

He let Rufus smell his hand, and then he pet him. Rufus enjoyed the attention.

"Nice dog. What's his name?"

"Rufus."

He chuckled. "Original." He stopped petting Rufus and said to me, "Mind cleaning up after the dog?"

"As soon as I get money to buy the pooper-scooper."

"You can pick it up with your hands and a plastic bag."

"Are you kidding?" Today was going to be a day for doggie gross-out, I could see it.

"You put your hand in the bag and pick up the poop. Turn the bag inside out and voila."

"No, thank you."

"Suit yourself." He shrugged and took a drag on the cigarette. "But we'd like the place to be a little clean for the neighbors."

"I'll see what I can do," I said. I let Rufus tug me away, as he was impatient to get out of the hot weather and get into the relatively cooler air conditioning.

I left the A/C on in the living room and left to go to the library to drop off one book I had read. After that, I walked down the hill to Scott's store.

He wasn't open. I checked my phone that had the time. It was 11:30, half an hour past the time he should be there.

I called him. He didn't answer. I closed the phone and looked in the direction of the parking garage. Maybe he was parking. I gave him a couple of minutes and tried again. Nothing.

Where could he be? Should I start walking to his house?

My phone rang. Scott. I picked up. "Where are you?"

"I'm at the hospital."

"What?" Oh, my God.

"I'm okay. It's Tyler."

Oh, dammit, really? "What's he there for?"

"Ralph's boyfriend got home early and they had a fight."

"So what are you doing there?"

He said, almost sounding like he spoke to someone dense, "I'm the only person he knows in the state. Other than you, of course."

As if I would go to the hospital for Tyler. "What about Ralph, huh?"

"Mike, he's my friend. I would do the same for you."

I knew he would. But sometimes, he was too kind, I thought. He should have let Tyler just rot, especially after leaving us the way he did.

"I'll be out of here as soon as I can."

"Fine," I said.

"We have to go back to Ralph's place and get Tyler's stuff. If the boyfriend didn't throw it all out."

"Come get me first." I wasn't going to leave Tyler alone with Scott anymore. "I'll be at home."

"Are you sure?"

"Yes," I said. I wasn't happy about it, but if I helped him, maybe he'd go away permanently.

"Okay. I'll call you."

I hung up, glaring at the phone. Then I looked up at the sky. "You're funny, you know that?"

ELEVEN

IT AIN'T OVER

A BOUT FIVE O'CLOCK, Scott picked me up in his truck. I sat next to Tyler, pushing aside the crutch. "What happened?" I asked Tyler as we drove to the highway.

"Got thrown down the stairs," he said, looking back at me. He had a black eye and scratches on his face. "Sprained ankle and wrist." He lifted his hand, which was wrapped with a brown elastic bandage. "Fractured ribs, ten stitches on my head."

"Geez." Yeah, I guess being thrown down the stairs would do that to you. "And we're going back there to get your stuff?"

"At least my car."

"How big is this boyfriend?"

Tyler looked away. "I don't think the three of us could take him."

Scott said, "We're not going to fight him. We're going to ask for your stuff and leave."

"Where are we going?" I asked.

"Jamestown."

I threw my head back against the cushion. Scott and I had gone to Newport and had to pass through Jamestown. It was a hike, and here I was, stuck next to an injured Tyler. I couldn't kick him when he was down, even if I wanted to.

We drove for quite a while. We ended up by the sea shore, in a small seaport. Tyler pointed to a big building with apartments that looked out onto the docks and a tiny beach.

When we arrived, we climbed out of the truck, Tyler leaning heavily on his right leg, his left leg encased in a black boot. He tucked the crutch under his left armpit. He took a breath. "Where's my car?"

"Maybe they moved it," said Scott. Then he asked me, "Think you'll be able to drive?"

"I don't know how to drive, Scott," I said, hoping to God I would not have to get behind the wheel of another car. Ever.

"Don't worry," said Tyler. "You're not driving my car."

I had no idea how he was going to drive with a sprained ankle, but I said nothing more as we crossed the street.

"I don't see it," Tyler said again, looking around.

"Where's the apartment?" I asked.

We walked a couple of yards in, and he stopped at the base of some wooden stairs. Tyler pointed up. "Second floor."

We went upstairs. "Second door in," he called. "205."

Scott took a breath and then knocked on the door. "Let me do the talking, Mike."

"Sure," I said, though if the guy was going to be a jerk, I was going to give it back.

I looked past the railing behind me. There was a patch of grass and a few walkways going through what could be considered a courtyard. Going down the stairs was probably not as bad as going over the railing, I thought.

The door opened. Dressed in only a pair of black shorts, the guy looked pissed. He was much older than me, probably in his thirties. Very well-built, easily a weight-lifter, he looked like some of the guys from prison. His long blond hair was tied up in a black thong.

"What?"

"We're Tyler's friends," Scott said. "We're just here to get his stuff."

The guy pointed beyond the railing. "It's down there. I threw it all out."

Scott backed up to the railing and glanced down. I didn't see anything on the ground.

"Tell him I towed his god damn car." He slammed the door in our faces.

Scott walked in front of me and headed to the stairs. "You sure you don't want me to talk to him?" I asked.

"No, Mike. Come on."

After debating whether or not to permanently lock the big guy inside his own apartment, I ended up following Scott to the base of the stairs.

"He did what?!" Tyler hobbled around Scott to the area below the apartment. "There's nothing here!"

Nope, not a thing. I walked around, and saw only crushed cigarette butts amid the grass.

"All my clothes … all my stuff. My car!"

Scott stood there, watching me walk around. There was really nothing I could do. I suppose I could have tried a finder's spell, but what if it was all in someone else's apartment?

"Somebody took your stuff," I said.

"No shit, Sherlock," stormed Tyler.

"Don't take it out on him," said Scott. "We have to find out who towed your car."

"I'll go ask," I said, heading to the stairs.

Scott put a hand on my arm. "I'll do it." He walked around to the front. I supposed that's where the building's office was.

Tyler sat on the steps. "God, this is horrible."

"Karma's a bitch," I said.

"What's that supposed to mean?" He glared up at me.

"You abandoned us at the club. We had to take a bus. I almost got into a fight on the way home. I'd say you deserve this."

"You're an ass." He turned his head from me, looking out at the grass in the courtyard.

Scott returned, finding me standing a far distance from him. Tyler looked at the grass in the courtyard. I looked in the opposite direction, out at the moorings, absently staring at the different types of boats docked there.

"I got the phone number of the tow company," Scott said, looking between the two of us.

"Can I borrow your phone?" asked Tyler.

"That got tossed out, too?" I asked.

"That, and my wallet, my keys, my money, everything."

"Great," I snarled.

Scott frowned.

Tyler took Scott's phone and called the number. "It's in the town yard? Where is that? Can you give me directions? I guess from downtown Jamestown." He listened carefully. "Got it, I think. Yes, I'm coming right now … Okay. Thanks."

He hung up and struggled up. "They're only going to be there for fifteen more minutes."

Scott asked, "You got the directions?"

"We get back on 138 and take the exit right before the bridge."

"Wait right here, I'll bring the truck around."

I jumped in the middle, caught the crutch, and Tyler climbed in next to me. Scott got back on the little highway and took the street before the bridge. Tyler gave directions, but they were confusing. We found ourselves at the water.

"I think we were supposed to go left back there," said Scott.

"Could have sworn she said right."

I sighed heavily and threw my head back against the cushion.

"Think you could have remembered it?" he yelled at me.

"I still know spells from when I was 12."

"Mike, stop," said Scott.

He sounded frustrated. He turned the truck around and we went back to where we were supposed to go left … and we got thoroughly lost. No matter where we went, the street ended at the water's edge. We had long passed the fifteen-minute window.

"I have a quarter of a tank of gas," said Scott. "We'll have to try and find it tomorrow."

Tyler winced. I guessed the painkillers were wearing off. We got back onto the highway, crossed the bridge, with the original steel Jamestown bridge right next to us. Scott took the first exit and got gas.

We then had to go to a pharmacy to get Tyler's pain pills. I waited in the truck. Tyler took a pill dry as he came out of the pharmacy.

"Let's get him to my house. Mike, can you help him?"

He had to climb three floors with that crutch. Scott went first, and I was behind Tyler, ready to catch him if he fell. By the time he got to the top, his t-shirt soaked through with his sweat.

We got him into the apartment and on the couch. Scott put on the air conditioner and told him he'd be right back.

We both got in the truck. Then both of us sighed. Scott turned to me.

"Sorry, Mike."

"It's not your fault."

"It's not his fault, either. Let it go."

"I'll try."

"Please."

I was silent. For him, I would try.

He put the truck in reverse and backed out of the driveway. "Are you sure you can't drive?"

"Driving wasn't a skill I needed in prison."

"You didn't even try it in the arcade or video games?"

"No, I was never into video games."

"We'll have to load him up with serious painkillers," Scott said with a sigh. "Will you come with us?"

"If you want me to go."

"We might need your help."

"Magical or mundane?" I grinned at him.

"Both." He didn't seem to look happy about it, though.

I thought about Tyler while I took Rufus for a walk that night. It really wasn't his fault. It was probably my fault. I wanted Tyler to leave, and he did. But Fate would not be denied by having him return to Scott.

Sometimes, you had to give in. Sometimes, like Scott said, you have to let it go. If I stopped pushing Fate's buttons, maybe Tyler would find a way to leave on his own.

Now, it looked like he was going to stick around a lot longer than I expected. I would have to get used to it and trust Scott.

Damn, that was hard.

The next morning at around seven, just as I got out of the shower, my cellular phone rang. The number was one I didn't know, but it had a local area code. I picked it up.

"Hello?"

"Grimaulkin," said Ritter's voice.

"Yessss," I replied, none too happy to hear him first thing in the morning.

"Be ready at three. We're going to investigate the Waters of Life."

"We are?"

"Yes."

"How are we going to do that?"

"They have a prayer meeting every Thursday night at five. We'll be there."

"Okay. Why do you need me?"

"Because you began this investigation."

"Hey, wait a minute, how did I start an investigation?"

But he hung up. I grumbled and made breakfast.

Scott called me an hour later on the house phone. "They'll be open at nine. I'll pick you up now. Can you help get him downstairs?"

"Sure," I said.

He picked me up, drove back to his house. We went down single-file, me in front in case Tyler fell. He held onto the railing with a death grip as he took one step at a time, and Scott carried his crutch.

He reached out with his left hand, still in the bandage, and took a hold of the crutch, before passing it to his right hand.

"Did some healing?" I said to Scott.

"I tried."

I got in the middle this time, and Tyler got in next to me. He kept his leg away from mine.

We were silent for a while, and then I said, "Look, Tyler …"

He turned to look at me.

"I'm sorry about what happened."

I think Scott almost swerved off the highway. Tyler blinked.

I continued, "If there's anything I can do …"

"Mike," asked Tyler. "You're apologizing?"

I shrugged.

He tried to put his left arm around my shoulders, but I backed off, bumping into Scott.

"That doesn't mean we're best friends."

Scott chuckled. Tyler said, "All right. I'll take what I can get."

It started to rain as we got closer to the bridge. Scott had gotten the directions this time and Tyler read them from a paper. We were able to find it in ten minutes.

The town junkyard was not a junkyard. It looked like a parking lot surrounded by a steel fence, with three cars parked in three spaces. There was a small, 4-by-4 guard house next to the gate. It wasn't open yet.

Scott looked at his phone. "It's nine."

"Figures," said Tyler. "My car's right there."

The rain came down. It started getting a little cramped in the truck. I didn't want to move and hit Tyler's left leg by mistake. And I didn't want to sit closer to Tyler than I had to.

Finally, another truck showed up, one with a seal on it that mirrored the steel monstrosity that was next to the bridge we crossed over. A woman got out, unlocked the fence and drove into the yard. We drove in after her.

She parked her truck as close to the shed as possible, got out and ran to its door, while we piled out into the rain. Tyler half-hopped to get out of the rain, while Scott and I walked behind him, getting more soaked with every step.

The woman was inside the shed. Tyler squeezed between the truck and the shed, which had a tiny awning over the door. There was no room for us, so Scott and I stood in the rain.

"I own the blue car over there."

The dark-skinned woman gave Tyler a once-over. "Okay."

"Can I take it?"

"Fifty dollars a day, and it's been here two days."

"It's only been here one day," Tyler argued.

"And a hundred dollars for the towing fee." She gave him a look that threatened she could tack on more fees if he was going to argue.

Scott noticed it and said, "Do you take Visa?"

"Does it look like I take Visa?" She motioned to the shed. There was nothing in it but a chair, a small black-and-white TV, a radio with a microphone, and a desk that was more like an extension of the windowsill. She at least had windows on all four sides.

"Cash only?"

"Yes."

Scott sighed. "I'll go to the bank."

"Wait," said Tyler. "Do you have the keys?"

"Came without keys," said the woman. "You sure you're the owner?"

"I lost all my ID's and got beat up."

She tsked. "Can't take it without an ID. It's Ontario plates. The police have to run it to make sure it's not stolen."

"But it's my car!"

She shrugged. "You have five days or it'll get towed to the mainland for scrap." She eyed him. "If it's not stolen."

Now, before yesterday, I would have thought "tough luck", but now, Scott was going to be out two hundred bucks, maybe more. This was hurting Scott, and that I could not abide.

I leaned into Scott and said, "Can we go back to the apartment, let me talk to the guy?"

Scott shook his head.

"Then let's go back there and I'll do a finder's spell."

Scott looked over at me, then nodded. "C'mon, Tyler. Let's go get the money."

Soaked from the rain, we went back to the truck. I told Tyler to go in first. "Scott's going to drop me off at the apartments, and I'm going to do a finder's spell."

"Can you do that?" asked Tyler.

"Sure," I said, though I had a better idea.

When Scott dropped me off on the side of the apartments, where we had gone in before, I told him, "Come back in about fifteen minutes, maybe more because of the rain."

"Mike —"

I ignored him as I dove out the door into the rain. I walked over to the stairs and glanced back. He was gone. Good.

I climbed the stairs, getting out of the worst of the rain because there was a third floor above it. I went to 205 and readied a blast spell. I knocked on the door.

It opened a crack. A small, round face peered out between the crack which extended a gold chain on the door. "Hello?" he said.

"You Ralph?"

He nodded.

"I'm Tyler's friend."

He started to shut the door. I held it open. "Do you have anything that belongs to him? His ID? His keys?"

Ralph looked down. "Wait." He ducked away from the door. I looked around, ready to blow my way in if I had to. He came back. A small, thin hand extended out a worn leather wallet. "Tom took the credit cards and shredded them and took the money."

I took the wallet and opened it. It had his license in there and an extra key that could have belonged to a house or a car for all I knew. Some pictures were in there as well. I closed the wallet. "Thank you."

I heard someone walking on the wood to the side of me. The big linebacker of a boyfriend crested the stairs.

"What're you doing here?" he yelled at me.

I took off running. He followed me, the bastard, as I ran the perimeter of the courtyard on the wooden second floor. I ran down the stairs on the other side of the courtyard and, as soon as I hit the grass, I poured it on and ran across the courtyard to the entrance.

I didn't check behind me. I ran out of the entrance, into the street. No cars were coming, so I crossed the street to the docks. I looked behind me then, seeing him stopped by a moving car that honked its horn at him.

In front of me were the docks. To my left was the beach, and my right was a series of shops. I took the right.

Just past the shops was a bank on the opposite side of the street. I aimed for the bank, not knowing if Scott would be there. I looked back to see the linebacker running sideways across the street toward me.

"Please be there, please be there ..." I prayed as I dashed across the street again to the bank. I saw Scott in the drive-up lane at the teller machine, pulling money out. Tyler hit him and pointed at me.

I ran past them to the back of the truck and vaulted into it. "Go! Go!"

The linebacker paused across the street as Scott peeled out of the drive-through. Again, no cars stopped us as we took a hard right and I rolled around in the bed of the truck. The middle of my back slammed into the wheel-well and I got soaked in the puddle that had gathered in the back of the truck.

I stayed hunkered down while Scott drove. Exposed in the back of the truck, the rain pelting down on me, with nothing to hold onto when he took turns, made me pretty damn miserable. I hoped Tyler appreciated this.

The truck stopped and I peered over the side. We were back in front of the town yard. I got out of the truck and handed Tyler his wallet.

He grinned broadly. "Mike, thank you!" He opened the wallet. His grin disappeared. "Where's my cards and my money?"

"The big guy shredded the cards and kept the money."

"That's just great!"

"At least you got your wallet back," said Scott, probably seeing the look on my face because I was going to clock Tyler any second now.

He snorted angrily and stormed over to the shack. Scott put a hand on my arm.

"Thank you, Mike."

I gave Scott a little smile and a peck on the cheek.

Meanwhile, Tyler was talking to the woman, and it started to get heated. She slammed the door on him and he returned to us.

Tyler said, spitting out rain as it flowed down his face. "They don't have keys for the car."

Scott asked, "Do you have any extra keys in the car?"

"No."

"Then we'll need a locksmith."

"You talk to her. I think I pissed her off."

Scott passed his hand through his hair, slicking it back, and went to the shack. As I stepped away from Tyler, I saw Scott under the awning, dialing a number on his cellular phone. He said something to the woman and came back to the truck.

"Get in. It'll be a while."

We steamed up the windows just by sitting there. Tyler showed us the pictures in his wallet, mostly of his family. There was one picture of him and Scott in front of a statue.

More than an hour later, a truck came in and parked behind us. Scott looked in the rear view mirror and said, "Here he is."

We got out again, the rain coming down in buckets. "Which car?" said the mechanic, whose shirt hung like a curtain over his gut.

"The blue Honda," said Tyler.

"You gonna be able to drive it?"

"I'll drive it."

The guy gave him the once over while Scott went to the shack. I followed the locksmith and Tyler to the car. The locksmith used a metal bar to pop open the door. The scent of burnt "grass" came out of the car.

The locksmith looked at the keyhole, nodded, and went back to his truck. Scott returned and we clumped together in the rain like wet rats. Scott handed Tyler a piece of paper. "Receipt," Scott said.

The man returned, and put a key in the ignition. The car started right up. He eyed Tyler as he climbed into the driver's seat. Scott looked at me. I raised my hands — I was not going behind the wheel.

"Please be careful with him, Mike."

"Don't go too fast."

The locksmith said, "Hey, a hundred dollars."

"I got it," said Scott, handing him the rest of the money in his hand.

"Need a receipt?"

"Yes."

I walked around the car with Scott and the locksmith. I separated from the two of them, going to the passenger side of Tyler's car. I climbed in.

Tyler stepped on the brake and put the car in gear, pulled out of the yard, past Scott and the locksmith.

"Hey, wait for Scott."

"I know where I'm going."

"Pull over."

"I'm getting out of here."

"Don't make me stop this car."

He glanced at me. I must've looked serious, though I was bluffing. He pulled over.

The locksmith's truck passed us first, then Scott, and we fell in behind him. We drove under the speed limit the whole way home. Tyler winced every once in a while. I noted that he used his right foot for both the brake and the gas. He didn't use the turn signals as we drove down the streets to Scott's place.

He parked on the street. We both were sweating because the air conditioning didn't work and both windows were up because of the rain.

"I need those pills," he said, throwing his head back against the seat.

"We just have to get you in the house," I said. "I'll help you."

"I'm in no condition to walk," he said, closing his eyes. "Just leave me here."

"I'll carry you," I said, getting out of the passenger's side before I changed my mind or heard him tell me no.

I opened the driver's side and put my arm around his back, tucked my other arm under his legs, and pulled him out slowly. Scott waited at his truck, and when he saw what I was doing, he rushed to open the apartment door.

"Is he okay?" he asked me, as we got into the house.

"In pain," said Tyler.

I carried him up the stairs, careful not to hit his left foot anywhere. I got him into the house and set him on the couch. "I'll get your crutches and stuff."

He nodded, while Scott got water from the faucet. His pills were on the coffee table, and he reached for them.

I retrieved his crutches and the key from the car, locked the door and went back upstairs. Tyler lay on the couch, pale and sweating. Scott had put the air conditioners on.

He looked worried. I walked up to him and put my arm across his shoulders. He was as damp as I was. "Why don't you take a hot shower," I told him. "I'll watch him."

"What about you?" he asked me.

"I'll be fine. I need to be back at my house by three."

"I have to open the store," he said.

"I can man the store until two-thirty if you want."

"You need a shower too."

"Well, thanks a lot."

He hugged me sideways. "Let me take a quick shower."

"We can take one together."

He chuckled and gave me a little shove. "What will you wear afterward?"

"Who says I have to wear anything?"

The store was dead in the rainstorm.

Two women came in and examined the stones that he had on display. I explained them. They smiled, and left without buying anything.

Then around quarter-past two, Ritter came in. He wore a long black coat along with his usual gray fedora. He wore a suit with even a tie under the coat.

"You're not going in that, are you?" he asked me, motioning to my t-shirt and jeans.

"I was going to change my shirt." I straightened out the counter. "I didn't expect to see you here."

He shrugged, walked around the store. "Nice place for you here. No temptations."

"None of the obvious ones, anyway."

He raised an eyebrow. He walked over to the small quartz crystal pebbles. He thrust his hand in the pile and pulled up one. Examining it in the palm of his hand, he said, "Fifty cents?"

"Yes."

He pocketed the stone, shuffled in his pocket for some change and pulled out some money in a money clip, bringing it to me. He peeled off a dollar bill. "Keep the change."

"Thanks, because I don't know how to open the cash register."

He snorted.

Scott's truck parked in front of the store and he got out. He ran to the door and came inside, stopping short at seeing Ritter.

"Oh, hello."

Ritter inclined his head.

I said, "Scott, meet Ritter."

Scott looked him over. He smiled, held out his hand. "Nice to meet you."

Ritter shook his hand, saying nothing. I'm sure Ritter must have read him with that one handshake.

"He'll be coming with me," said Ritter, letting go of Scott's hand.

"Let me go home and change my shirt." I looked at Scott. "How's Tyler?"

"Passed out. I came to bring you home, but if you've already got a ride …"

I glanced at Ritter. "Yeah."

"Call me?" Scott asked, as I came out from behind the counter.

I stopped in front of him. I didn't care that Ritter was there. I kissed Scott gently. "I will."

Ritter held the door open for me. "Take a left," he said. "The car's in the parking garage."

He made the car beep and the doors unlock from a distance by pressing a button on his keyring. I got in the passenger side. I put my seatbelt on.

"So?" I asked.

"So, what?"

"What do you think about him?"

"I think if you stick with him, he'll be good for you."

I guess that was as close to an endorsement as I was going to get.

"Tell me about the Waters of Life," Ritter said as he drove.

So I repeated to him, pretty much verbatim, what I had told the Knight.

"He called you by name?" Ritter asked.

"The Hebrew pronunciation. *Meye-KAY-el.*"

Ritter listened to me continue: what the reverend had done to me, calling me Legion, and what he had done to my cousin, and saying I could be free to have any woman. "It wasn't until then that the spell broke."

"I'd have to see him at work," said Ritter, "to see what kind of magic he's using."

"Maybe he's a medium?"

"Something's feeding him the information. I have to see what it is."

"Can you do that?"

"I'm surprised you can't."

"Not without help."

He glanced at me. "You expect me to give you permission to use a demon's power in a church?"

I tried to look innocent.

"Tell me," Ritter said. "How do you think you'd be able to do that?"

"If he's using demon powers to do what he can do."

"Not all helpful spirits are demons."

"Can't say I've met any."

"Maybe you should try."

I snorted. "Angelic powers? With me?"

"God forgives easily. All you have to do is approach with an open heart and willing mind."

"That might work for you. I seem to remember us having these discussions before."

"Often," he said. "And you gave me the same answer every time."

My answer was usually something akin to, *I don't need forgiveness.* Because I knew that I would get out of that prison and be one of the most powerful wizards in the world with all the knowledge that Grimalkin and I had. I'd be more powerful than the Rosicrucians and all their Knights put together. I'd be more powerful than the demons. I'd be on par with God.

Boy, was I young and stupid.

"Do you still stand by that answer?"

"I don't know," I whispered.

He heard me. He only nodded once and we were silent the rest of the way.

The rain pelted us as we approached the soaking wet meadow that surrounded the tent. People gathered inside the tent in a tight knot around the podium. Not as many people attended this prayer meeting as the Sunday service. These people were probably the diehards of the church.

I could see my Aunt Sue in the group. She caught and held my eye for a long time, said something to a woman she was talking to, and then came my way.

"Michael," she said, giving me a cold kiss on the cheek. "Whatever brings you here?"

"Brought a friend," I said, nodding to Ritter.

"Uncle Andy should be speaking tonight."

"Not the Reverend?"

"Oh, he'll be here, too. You are?"

"Ritter," he said, holding out his hand. My aunt shook it.

"Come sit with us," she said, looking up at Ritter's gray eyes.

"We'll sit on our own, thank you," Ritter said. He led me to a bench to the right of the podium. Most of the congregants had gathered at the left.

I listened to the pitter-patter of the rain on the tent, and hoped it wouldn't blow in on us. Someone thought to light kerosene lanterns. Everyone carried Bibles. Unprepared again.

One man got up from the knot of people and approached the podium. I hadn't seen him at the Sunday service. "I'd like to welcome you to the Waters of Life," he said. "Today we are first studying Psalm 31."

He opened his Bible and read the passage. "In You, oh Lord, I put my trust. Let me never be ashamed. Deliver me in Your righteousness. Bow down Your ear. Deliver me speedily. Be my rock of refuge. A fortress of defense to save me ..."

Although I had read the Bible a few times in prison, I hadn't memorized it. Ritter might have, for all I knew, but he sat impassive.

The man at the podium expressed his opinion of the Psalm, and other people commented. Ritter and I watched the people commenting, like a tennis match. When that conversation got boring, another person got up and spoke, using a different reading.

So it was, for about an hour, reading and discussing scripture. I tried to pay attention. Finally, out of the group of people, Reverend Greene stepped out. Ritter sat up straighter.

"Isiah 51," he began, and looked right at Ritter. "Listen to Me, you who follow after righteousness. You who seek the Lord. Look to the rock from which you were hewn, and to the hole of the pit from which you were dug."

Reverend Greene smiled at Ritter. "What does that mean to you?" he asked Ritter.

"Pay attention to my past," Ritter replied.

"If you learned from the past, you can know the future. You already know the present. You embrace the present and live thoroughly within it. The past is what drives you." Greene looked at me. "Both of you."

Then he turned to the congregation. We were dismissed as he went off into something else. Ritter sat and watched him, while I watched Ritter. I didn't pay attention to Greene as he addressed his congregation, concentrating on Ritter for the most part.

Then we all sang Hosanna which I vaguely knew but Ritter knew well. We looked out at the dark past the tent. The rain had eased up.

I looked at Ritter as we walked back to the car. We got in.
"Well?"
"He's the real deal."
"You mean he's Jesus?"

"No." He pulled out of the parking spot and onto the muddy road. "He's been touched by God." He sighed. "We have to watch him."

"Why?"

"Because those touched by God usually go insane."

TWELVE

THE SHOE DROPS

I TOOK RUFUS OUT IN THE DARK WHEN I GOT HOME. I thought about calling Becky. I would do a final check when the ad ran to make sure that Carabesi's place was busy this weekend, and then I'd be done with the Mafia stalking her. No longer would I have to worry about the pastor from the church. The Rosicrucians would take care of it now.

Tyler was someone I was going to have to deal with until he healed up and went on his way back to Toronto. In three days, Dom and Evie would be coming back, and I would have to look into trying to find a real job and get an apartment. Maybe Frank would let me sleep in his office.

I got back to the apartment. Just after eight o'clock, I called Becky.

She answered on the second ring. "Hello!"

"You sound perky."

She giggled. "Hi, Mike. I aced my test."

"That's great! How much longer do you have to go to school?"

"For this? Three more weeks."

"It'll be over before you know it and you'll graduate at the top of your class."

"I only get a certificate."

"You'll get an A-plus. I know you will."

She sighed. "Then I have to find a job."

"I can help with that."

"You know people?"

I laughed. "You could say that."

"Don't get in trouble."

"I promise, I won't. Call me next week, okay?"

"Okay, Mike. Thank you so much for helping me out."

I felt a glow in my chest. "You're welcome, Becky."

I then called Scott. Tyler was passed out again, Scott was lonely and we talked for a while. I told him that I would go watch the store in the afternoon if he wanted me to, after I went to the library to check my mail.

I went to bed, knowing things had been solved.

Friday morning, I cleaned. Probably not as well as Evie, but I did my best. I put away the sheets that were on the couch, straightened up, vacuumed, and cleaned the bathroom. The house smelled like lemons. I felt like I had accomplished something. I left Rufus and walked over to the library.

I got coffee for the girls first, then dipped behind the Congressional Records to see if there was anything. Nothing, as I expected, then headed to Scott's store.

Scott gave me a wan smile. "How are you?"

"Good," I said, giving him a kiss. "Everything's nice and quiet."

"That means a shoe is going to drop with a really big thud."

"What kind of shoe?"

"I don't know. Just a feeling." He sighed. "I do know that this stuff Tyler's taking is really powerful. An hour after he takes it he's out for three hours."

"That's good for you, isn't it?"

Scott shrugged. "I guess. But not good if he gets addicted to it. Then he'll never go home."

I didn't like that idea. "He won't get addicted."

"I hope not." He came out from behind the counter. "I unlocked the cash register this time. I'll take you out to China Inn when I pick you up."

I smiled. "Okay."

I waved goodbye to him and took my position behind the counter.

A little while later, some kids came in: three young men, all together in a clump. They separated as soon as they walked in, one heading to the stones, another to the herbs, and the third to me.

I knew what they were trying to do, distract me. If anyone was going to steal anything, it would be the stones. They were small and numerous, easy to pluck and put in a pocket. They might have been cheap, but enough could disappear to cause a problem with the inventory.

The kid who came up to me asked, "Hey, you got bat's blood?"

"This isn't that kind of store," I said.

"I heard this was a magic store."

"New Age store." I looked beyond the kid. "Put that back."

The other kid flushed and put the malachite stone that he had dropped into his pocket back on the table. "C'mon, Jimmy, let's get outta here."

"You creeped out?" said the kid who came up to me. He leered at me.

The kid near the stones left. The one near the herbs looked like he wasn't sure whether to stay or go. Jimmy gave him a look.

I said, "If you're thinking of stealing, or something worse, that would be a bad idea."

"What're you gonna do about it? Three on one."

"Two. Soon to be even."

The kid turned around and saw that the kid with the stones left. I leaned forward on the counter. The kid near the herbs must not have liked the look I was giving the other kid, because he left.

The speaker watched him go. "Ready to rumble, kid?" I said, cracking my knuckles.

"You don't scare me."

"Oh, but I should." I opened my hand and willed a small flame in my palm.

The kid gasped, staring at it, and took off.

Too easy.

China Inn was crowded, but we got a table in the corner where things were relatively quiet. Scott sipped his water with lemon and sat back.

"We just got Tyler's appointments for follow-ups. Not for another month."

"How's he going to pay for it?"

"He's on the Canadian health plan. I don't know how they're going to handle it. He might leave before then. I hope he does."

I chuckled. "I could probably spell for it."

"You already did that. Look at where it got him."

I shut up and drank my soda. We ate our dinner and he dropped me off at home, giving me a kiss that tasted of sweet and sour sauce.

I took Rufus out and, by the time I got home, the room had cooled off. I fed him, sat down on the couch, and scanned through TV, settling on a documentary on the mystic origins of the SS in Germany during World War II.

I had left my phone charging on the counter, and it rang. I jumped up and got it. It was Becky's number.

"Mikey!"

"Becky?"

"Help me — ow!" I heard a slam, a bang, a thud, and screaming.

"Becky!"

The screaming faded, as I heard more slams. Then, nothing.

"Becky!"

Nothing. I picked up the cordless phone and called Scott. No answer. I called Frank. No answer there either. I kept yelling for Becky on the cellular phone, but no one answered me.

I looked at the keys in the bowl by the door. The keys that belonged to Dom and Evie's car.

I knew how to get there. Take the highway. The highway. In the car.

Calling Scott again, I saw Belial in the black armor and shining eyes through the helmet standing at the door. He pointed to the keys in the bowl. "Take them."

Scott didn't answer. I hung up. Slowly, I plucked the keys from the bowl. I saw the key to the house, a copy of the one I carried. I saw a couple of smaller keys, one round, one square.

"Screw it," I said, and threw open the door, shattering Belial.

Rufus got up, but I was out the door before he crossed the floor to the door.

I ran downstairs and used the small round key to unlock the door to the car. The square key fit in the ignition.

"Help me, please," I whispered and turned the key. The car started up, no problem. I put the car in R, which I assumed was reverse, and it backed up a tiny bit. I kept my foot on the brake as I backed out into the street, praying nobody would come out.

I backed into the middle of the street. I shifted the car into D and the car jerked forward. Again, my foot on the brake, I let it crawl forward.

I held onto the steering wheel tightly, my back ramrod straight and looking directly out the windshield. I had to get on the highway. First I had to get through four stop lights.

I knew I couldn't crawl like this on the highway. I found my way to the entrance ramp onto I-95.

"Watch your side mirrors," came Belial's voice as I drove onto the highway.

There were hardly any cars, but I watched the mirror, and no one came up on my right-hand side. Looking back out of the front windshield, I concentrated on what was in front of me. I had to drive to 495 and get the exit there. When I got onto 495, traffic slowed down, eventually to a crawl.

"Oh, come on!"

As I followed the traffic, tapping the brakes every few feet, I don't know what caused the clog by the time I got through it. Instead I found myself behind someone going 40.

Belial said, "Put your signal light on."

I turned the button for the headlights.

"No, the arm on the left. Push it down."

I pushed it down, and the signal light blinked toward the left.

"When it is clear in your mirror, move to the other lane."

I looked in the left-hand mirror. No one seemed to be coming, so I poured on the speed and bolted into the other lane. I got the hint, and passed the slow-moving car. I was sweating and terrified.

I tilted the arm up, the signal light pointed right. I drove into the other now empty lane.

There were two exits to go.

I got off the exit, and again sat up straight. I had to remember to use the signal lights when I was turning. So many things to remember while driving!

I drove down her street and stopped across the street from her house. I put the gear into P, turned the car off and tried to calm my racing heart with deep breaths, passing my hand through my sweat-drenched hair. Finally, the shakes stopped and I got out of the car, taking the keys out of the ignition, then crossed the street.

Becky's car sat in her driveway. I tried the door that led into the house her apartment was in — it opened. The lock was broken. I went upstairs to her apartment, and her door was wide open.

"Becky!" I called, knowing she wasn't there, but on the off chance someone was in the house.

I stepped on something and cracked it — her phone. I picked it up and put it in my pocket. Maybe I could still use it, since I had left my phone at home. I checked all the rooms. Nothing was gone, just the kitchen area had been tussled, with chairs knocked over.

"Do a finder's spell," said Belial, standing at the doorway to Becky's bathroom. "I can help."

"You can help if I summon you, and I know better than that."

He shrugged. "This is the chance that you would have to take."

I was going to use his suggestion to do a finder's spell, however. I went into the bathroom and found her brush. I pulled three long strands of hair from it and tied it into a loop. In her bedroom, I found what I needed: a thin, silver chain. I looped the hair through the chain, put my will into it, and said, "Find my match."

Holding it like a pendulum, the hair, even though it was physically light, psychically pulled the chain to my left. I turned to the left, and it pulled the chain out directly in front of me.

I left the apartment and tested the pendulum outside. I oriented myself by the North Star, and the pendulum pointed west. When I got in the car, I put the silver chain around the rear view mirror.

I found myself back on the highway, checking the pendulum every few minutes. A car passed me, so close that I could almost feel him sort of pull me toward him as he passed. I held tight to the steering wheel. People continued to pass me, but I was going the speed limit.

I had to get off at route 126, the next exit. I followed that until I got to 146, and the pendulum swung wildly to the right.

I didn't need the pendulum. I knew where I was going.

To the Tabernacle.

I had to drive going ten miles an hour, in the dark, with the high-beams bobbing and weaving at every pothole on the dirt road to the Tabernacle. I came over the rise and saw the Tabernacle in its naked, exposed form in the waxing moonlight. The white tent was still up, though there were no lights anywhere except for my high-beams.

I saw three vehicles parked near the tent. The pendulum swung in a circle. I had found her, but where?

I got out of the car, pocketing the keys. Stumbling in the dark, I walked past the tent. A satellite dish was set up there, along with a box-truck that I walked into the side of. I felt my way around it, my eyes still adjusting to the lack of light.

I could see a flickering light a just ahead of me. I followed it, going out into a meadow, carefully stepping around potholes and bumps.

"Here he comes," I heard someone say.

Someone raised the light, and I could see four people standing around. Becky who sat on a crate. She wore a thin nightgown and didn't look at me. Three were men, big men. The last one was Reverend Greene. He held a black book in his hand. A Bible, most probably.

He stepped forward. "I knew you would find us," he said.

"What's all this about?" I asked. "Let Becky go."

"I will let her go, but you are who we want." He opened the book, and said, "Exodus 22:18. Thou shalt not suffer a witch to live."

"Me?" I said. I laughed. "I'm not a witch, I'm —"

Two men had flanked me while we were talking, and now grabbed me. I struggled, as they yanked my arms behind me, throwing me a little off balance. I lashed out with my feet, connecting with someone who swore at me and then danced out of the way of a follow-up kick.

Someone clocked me on the side of the head with his fist, and I jerked sideways. I tried to pull my arm free, but they held it fast, and, in fact, tied both arms up behind me.

They shoved me forward, and someone tripped me so I fell face-first into the dirt. I turned my head to see Becky, crying. Her hands were tied behind her, too. They grabbed my legs, tied my ankles together. Someone gagged me as I tried to make motions with my hands to start a spell. They wrapped rope around my hands, then I was hog-tied, ankles to wrists. They tilted me sideways and tied another rope around my waist. At the end of the rope, they had an O-ring, which they threaded a chain through. At the end of the two-link chain was a large concrete block about as big as my torso.

They had obviously read *Malleus Maleficarum*, or *The Witches' Hammer*, a 16th-century tome that witch hunters at the time used to "test" people for witchcraft. One of the common tests was to weigh the person down with stones and throw them into a river. If they came back up, they were a witch. If they stayed down, they weren't. But then, they were also dead.

Now, I was a magician, but I was not a stage magician, and couldn't get out of a trick like this. Houdini probably could do something to get his hands free; but me, no.

Two men picked up the concrete block, and the other one manhandled me, half-dragging me through the meadow. Becky was screaming, "Stop it!" She was cut off suddenly by a slap, probably by the Reverend.

They dragged me a short distance to the banks of a stream. The men with the concrete block walked out into the stream, which I could see flowed up to their thighs. They dropped the block, and I fell in, face first, my hands and feet outside of the water. It was more like stagnant water, that's how slow it moved.

I had tried to take a deep breath, but when the concrete block dropped, it jerked me down and into the water with a splash. Water flowed into my mouth through the gag, and I tried to spit it out. I tried not to breathe.

Belial didn't appear, because I couldn't summon him. Grimalkin did, though, his black hooves in the water.

This is how it will end, I thought: my last sight the black hooves of the demon that guided me.

Help me!

He bent down, his face in the water, level with mine. "Send me home," he said.

Yes, now help me!

"You promised. You lied. You will send me home when you get out of this."

My vision started to get dark around the edges and my lungs burned. I would have to send him home. I knew what I needed to do.

You need medication and psychotherapy. We can help you get rid of the voices.

As soon as I thought of that, he rose.

A moment later, I felt someone tug at my wrists and ankles, turning me sideways. They dragged me, and the concrete block, through the water. I could feel air on my face, caught a couple of bursts of fresh air through my nose before I was dunked under again.

Finally I crested the water, and someone kicked me in the back as they slid down the bank. "Mikey," called Becky.

I muttered something through the gag.

"Oh, thank God," she said. She rolled and I felt her hands awkwardly hold mine for a few seconds, then her fingertips tugged at the rope around my hands. She couldn't undo that knot.

I tried to talk through the gag, but the spell came out garbled and didn't work. She moved her hands down to my face, and pushed the gag down enough so I could get out a word, "Untie!"

The word and my will loosened the ropes. She got them off her wrists, and I lay down with the concrete block below my stomach. I took great gulps of air. Finally, I moved my hands to my face and shoved down the gag.

"Thank you," I said to Becky.

"I don't know when they'll be back," she said. I hugged her through the cold, wet nightgown.

I shoved the rope from my waist, leaving the concrete block there. I helped her up the banks of the stream. I checked my pockets. The keys were still in there, and Becky's phone in my other pocket had been soaked, unusable now.

"C'mon, we have to get to the car."

I took her hand, and started half-jogging, half-running to the tent, the clearest thing I could see in the distance.

I heard voices.

"They're back," she said.

I realized that, but I didn't let go of her hand. "We'll get there first," I said.

I tripped on something, and struggled when I got up. Becky helped me up. I took her hand again and we ran around the tent, keeping to the shadows.

Then headlights flashed on, illuminating the right side of the tent. We were approaching from the left side. A lantern turned on near the satellite dish. We skirted that, kept to the left side of the tent, while people yelled for Becky.

The lights from the headlights were too bright, so we went around them. The voices headed away from us, going back to the meadow I had entered. They would find the concrete block soon enough.

We got to one of the vehicles with the headlights on. A full-sized pickup, it was larger than the Camry. It was open. The keys were in the ignition.

"Get in," I said. Becky climbed in the driver's seat, I went around to the passenger's side from the back.

This one had a shifter on the floor. 1, 2, 3, 4, 5, and R. This was like Scott's old truck. I looked down at the floor; there were three pedals there instead of two. I remembered Scott used to press on the third pedal and lift it up slowly when he was at a stop. Becky stared at the shifter. "I don't know how to drive a standard," she said.

"Quick, switch places."

I got out and, when I did, someone tackled me, forcing the door closed and slamming it into my side. I grunted, shoved the door open, away from me. Becky screamed and locked the door on her side.

I stepped out from between the door and the truck, shutting the door with a slam. I yelled at Becky, "Keep the door locked!"

Someone tried to throw a lantern at my head, but I ducked, and it hit the window of the truck. The windshield and lantern shattered. I backed up, going around to the back of the truck. Red lights illuminated where I stood when Becky stepped on the brake, and then white lights when she threw the truck into reverse.

She must have figured out the third pedal.

I was directly behind the truck, and she floored it. I jumped onto the bumper and vaulted into the bed, as she churned dirt and backed the truck up fast enough to run over a screaming bump. The truck slammed into one of the pillars of the Tabernacle.

I rolled around in the bed of the truck, getting slammed into the tailgate. I heard her grinding gears. I struggled up and got to the window in the back of the truck. I pounded on it.

"Put it into first and use the clutch!" I yelled, repeating Grimalkin's voice in my head.

I felt the truck engage into first gear and lurch forward, almost throwing me out of the back. I held onto the rear window as we bumped along the meadow, the truck whining loudly in first gear.

"Clutch, shift down!"

She either didn't hear me, or didn't understand me, because we whined all the way out of the meadow.

We got onto the road and Becky pulled over, the truck coasting to a stop on the shoulder. I heard her put the emergency brake on and shut off the truck.

I climbed out of the truck bed and she opened the door. We were both shaking, but she wasn't crying.

"Do you know how to drive this?"

"I've seen Scott drive one. I think I can drive it."

"We need to go to the police," she said.

"I have something better. Let's get to a phone."

We climbed back into the truck. I felt better about driving this truck, even if it was a behemoth. Up ahead was a gas station with a convenience store.

I pulled into a parking spot. There was a phone booth. I searched in the truck for change. I found some in the ash tray.

I called the number the gray Knight had given me.

He answered the phone. "Hello?"

"Did I wake you?"

"Yes. Grimaulkin?"

"Yes. It seems that the Waters of Life is more like a Waters of Death."

I gave him a fast description of what had happened to Becky and me. "Where are you right now?" he asked me.

"At a Shell gas station. I don't know what road this is."

"Stay where you are. We will send a Pathfinder to get you." A Pathfinder was similar to a walking finder's spell, a psychic bloodhound.

"What if the Reverend comes to find us?"

"I am contacting the Knights right now. Stay where you are." He hung up.

We got back in the truck. "They're sending someone to come get us."

"The guy behind the counter keeps staring at us."

If he called the police, it wouldn't matter, because I had just called the magic police. I didn't like sitting here, waiting. I felt like we were sitting ducks.

A car that could best be described as a muscle car pulled into the gas station: orange with a black stripe down the middle of its hood. Its driver revved the engine before shutting it off. I could see a bunch of guys in the car, piling out one after the other to go inside the store, while the driver started pumping gas.

Then another car, a simple silver sedan, pulled in and parked directly behind us.

"That's the car they put me in," Becky said.

We rolled up the windows in our truck. Two men got out of the car. The man on the driver's side started stalking up to my door, while the one on the passenger's side walked up to Becky's side.

He stood about a foot away from the door. I looked down, grabbed the handle, and lifted, then kicked the door open. It slammed into him, making him stumble back. The second man ran around the front of the truck.

"Keep the doors locked!" I told Becky as I got out and slammed shut the door. I heard her lock the door.

The second man cleared around the front and I raised my hand, yelling, "*Explosio!*"

The air boomed, and both men flew backward across the ten yards from the truck to the convenience store. One man fell into the air compressor, the other against the wall. They bounced off and fell face-first onto the tarmac.

I felt the magic humming through me. I could finish them off. They hurt Becky. I clenched my fists and advanced on them. They tried to kill me. They deserved to —

"Mikey, no!" Becky threw open the door, tripped over something and fell on me, making me stumble sideways. The magic faded immediately, breaking my concentration to send another spell at them.

What was I doing?

I exhaled, put my arm around Becky's waist and stood straighter. The guys from the orange car stood at the door of the convenience store.

"Let's get back in the truck."

Then a black van pulled into the gas station, coming right at me. I put Becky behind me and faced the headlights, readying a spell.

It stopped right in front of me with a short squeal of tires. Four men came out of the van, all of them in black suits. Knights.

They pulled Becky away from me.

"Mikey!"

They shoved me against the truck.

"Easy!" I yelled.

I was frisked, yanked to the black van. Becky was seated in the back seat, a Knight next to her, closing the door. I was shoved in, a Knight next to me.

Without a word, they pulled out of the gas station, did an illegal U-turn, and headed back up the highway.

"Turn here," I said.

They did, and we bounced through the meadow. I saw the Camry. We continued past the Camry to the tent, past that to the back meadow, where five other black vans were parked in a circle.

We tucked in between two vans. Doors slid open, and one of the Knights helped Becky out. I climbed out.

Men swarmed around the Tabernacle. Others were at the stream. The Reverend was nowhere to be found.

A short time later, Becky sat at the van, a blanket around her. I sat with her, waiting. I saw four Knights posted at each of the four directions, probably unconsciously. A group of Knights showed up from the banks of the river, carrying a chain.

Dawn broke over the horizon. I yawned, leaned against the door. Becky leaned against me. I didn't even feel my eyes close.

I felt someone shake me. I opened my eyes, jerking up straight, waking Becky. I looked into Ritter's gray eyes.

"We found the block," he said. "And the ropes."

I rubbed my eyes. "Did you find Greene?"

"No. We saw the damage to the building." He stood up straight. "Want us to take you home?" He looked from me to Becky.

Becky nodded.

"I have to bring back the car," I said.

Ritter looked at the tent. "That car?" He motioned beyond the tent.

"If you could get someone else to drive it —"

"How did you get it here?"

"I drove it. But I don't like to drive."

"I'll get someone to drive you."

The Knight who drove me was the Pathfinder. He was quiet, didn't ask me how to get home, but drove down the highway as if he had gone this way all his life. I didn't know if I could talk to him, if I would disturb his ability.

He parked the car in the driveway and exited the car. "Good luck."

"Thanks."

"Mind if I use your door?"

"Uh, sure."

He walked up the short steps to the side door. He stood there, turned the doorknob, and opened the door. I could see beyond just white light, and he stepped through it. The door shut behind him.

I walked up to the door and opened it. It led to the stairs in front of me, the door to the first-floor apartment next to that.

It must have been teleportation magic. Son of a gun. I was told it was unreliable unless you were a sensitive. I had no idea Knights knew that.

I left the apartment with Rufus and looked over at the driveway. There, sitting next to the beat-up Camry, was a brand-new white Cadillac with a license plate frame from Herb's Cadillac.

I grinned.

THIRTEEN

EPILOGUE

I SLEPT UNTIL ABOUT NOON and, when I got up, I fed Rufus and myself, then I took the bus to Providence. I had seen the parking situation in Downtown, and knew I would never be able to park the Camry there.

I walked up the hill to the Atheneum. I didn't know if the Knight in gray was going to be there, but I had to try. I had promised Grimalkin.

I opened the door to the Atheneum and the sergeant there took note of me. "He's been expecting you," he said.

"Thanks," I said, and walked to the back of the library. He sat reading a book on his lap and wearing glasses. He looked at me over the glasses.

"Ah, Grimaulkin." He closed the book and set it aside. "We heard about the business with the Waters of Life."

I nodded. "That's not what I'm here for."

"What is it, then?"

I sat down in the chair across from him. "Ritter said I would need therapy and medication to get rid of the voices."

He tilted his head.

"I'm ready for that." I looked steadily at the Knight in the gray suit. "I'm ready to send Grimalkin home."

ABOUT THE AUTHOR

Find out more about the world of L. A. Jacob at *Grimalkin's Grimoire* (grimaulkin.com) and *Dark Mystic Quill* (darkmysticquill.com)

YOU MIGHT ALSO ENJOY

GRIMAULKIN

by L. A. Jacob

Treading the straight and narrow is not natural to one who summons demons.

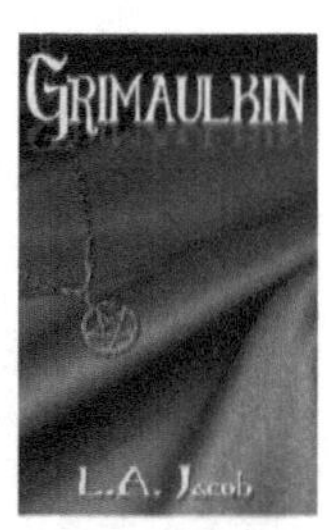

HOMECOMING
A War Mage Novel

by Jake Logan

Even wizards in the U.S. armed forces have to go home some time.

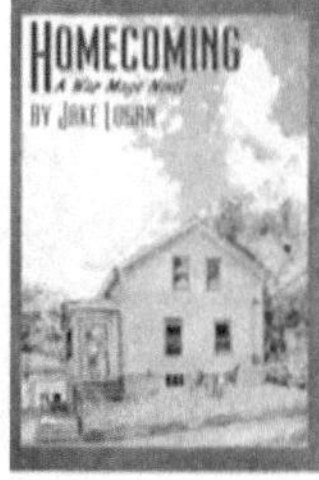

Best Intentions
Book One of the Glass Bottles Series

by J Dark

When your past is left undone, it will come find

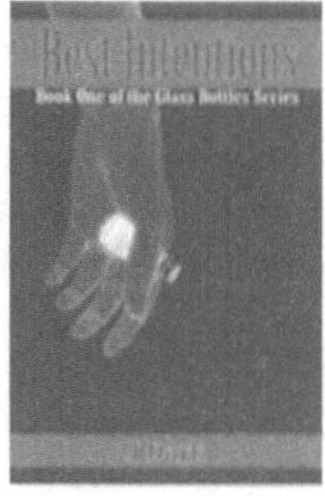

Available from Paper Angel Press
in hardcover, trade paperback, ebook, and audio editions.
paperangelpress.com